Arthur Henry Adams

Napoleon

A play in four acts

Arthur Henry Adams

Napoleon
A play in four acts

ISBN/EAN: 9783337350604

Printed in Europe, USA, Canada, Australia, Japan

Cover: Foto ©Andreas Hilbeck / pixelio.de

More available books at **www.hansebooks.com**

NAPOLEON

A Play in Four Acts

BY

HENRY A. ADAMS, M.A.

———

NEW YORK

J. SELWIN TAIT & SONS

65 FIFTH AVENUE

1894

TO MY WIFE.

PREFACE.

In the development of the play, I have availed myself as little as possible of "poetic license." The scenes occur, without exception, exactly in the order, and at the time and place assigned to them in History.

With the exception of *Babette*, all of the characters are historical personages; for even *Imperator*, the shade of Charlemagne, was seen on more than one occasion by *Napoleon*—in his dreams. His faith in the entire accountability of such appearances is undisputed, and he has told us that the impressions made upon his mind by vivid presentations of dead men, and other unsubstantial fancies of his brain, had much to do in shaping his career and fostering his views on Destiny. Just before the battle of Arcole, Napoleon saw Josephine's spirit distinctly, says Saint-Amand.

Beyond the necessary grouping of the dialogues and incidents within the practicable limits of stage scenes, I feel that I have not done History much violence.

As will appear by my brief " Outlines of the Characters," and numerous appended notes, the sentiments and traits, and frequently the very language, attributed to the *dramatis personæ*, rest upon good authority.

The *Memoirs* of Mme. de Rémusat, Mme. de Staël, the Duchess of Abrantès, Bourrienne, Pasquier, Constant, Imbert de Saint-Amand, Marmont, Ségur, Las Cases, O'Meara, etc., etc., have been minutely studied, no less than the more formal works of standard historians. Quite naturally, the *Memoirs* prove for the playwright the richer mine, their higher colouring and more familiar details giving the portraits painted the touch of life.

Napoleon has figured on the stage for half a century, but until very recently he has been made to cut a sorry figure, being the central person, merely, in pieces purely spectacular—or, still worse, the grotesque swashbuckler of more serious plays.

The sudden and widespread revival of interest this year, bids fair to call from the French dramatists of note some great Napoleon. Meanwhile, an humble fellow-craftsman offers this modest effort.

H. A. A.

Questover Lodge, Christmas, 1893.

CAST OF CHARACTERS.

NAPOLEON..................... *Emperor of the French.*
LUCIEN BONAPARTE.......... *Brother to Napoleon.*
JOSEPH BONAPARTE.......... *Brother to Napoleon.*
TALLEYRAND .... *Minister of Foreign Affairs.*
FOUCHÉ .... *Minister of Police.*
PIUS VII ... . *The reigning Pope.*
CAULAINCOURT ....*Duke of Vicenza.*
NEY ⎫
....*Marshals of France.*
MACDONALD ⎭
CONSTANT .... *Valet to Napoleon.*
YVAN .... *A Court Physician.*
RUSTAN ... . *A Mameluke Slave.*
CARDINAL FESCH .... *Uncle to Napoleon.*
IMPERATOR.................... *An Hallucination.*
JOSEPHINE .... *Empress of the French.*
COUNTESS WALEWSKA.......... *Mistress to Napoleon.*
HORTENSE.................... *Step-daughter to Napoleon.*
MME. DE RÉMUSAT............. *A Lady in-Waiting.*
MME. MURAT .... *Sister to Napoleon.*
BABETTE...... .... *A Chambermaid.*

       Pages, Attendants, etc., etc.

THE SCENES.

ACT I. : 1804. AT BAY.

SCENE 1 : The Library at Malmaison.
SCENE 2 : The Pavilion of Flora at the Tuileries.

ACT II. : 1807. HIGHNOON AND AFTER.

SCENE 1 : A Private Room at Finkenstein Castle.
SCENE 2 : A Terrace at Fontainebleau.

ACT III. : 1809. THE EVENING SACRIFICE.

SCENE 1 : A Secret Boudoir at Saint-Cloud.
SCENE 2 : A Gallery at Fontainebleau.

ACT IV. : 1814. THE SHADOW OF DEATH.

SCENE 1 : A Bed-room at Malmaison.
SCENE 2 : A Bed-room at Fontainebleau.

THE STORY.

"THE Emperor had just been proclaimed. . . .
The curtain has risen, the play begins, and no drama
is fuller of contrasts, of incidents, of movement.
The leading actor, *Napoleon*, was already as familiar
with his part as if he had played it since his child-
hood. *Josephine* is also at home in hers. . . .
The minor actors are not so accustomed to their new
positions."[1]

So writes M. Imbert de Saint-Amand, whose vividly
dramatic style has done so much toward making the
people and the scenes of the Napoleonic era realities
to us. The brief magnificent decade of the First
Empire came to an end. The Emperor, deserted,
stung with the unendurable sense of failure and
dashed and ruined hopes, must abdicate. The Marshals must return with the news of doom. They
come. The little bed room on the second floor at
Fontainebleau becomes the scene of what, dramati-
cally speaking, is the real end. More than one
writer has so declared it. M. de Bourrienne, *Napoleon's* private secretary, says in his Memoirs: "Such
was this night-scene, which possessed more dramatic

---

[1] The Court of the Empress Josephine (Scribner's), page 4.

effect than many which are performed on the stage ; on its *dénouement* depended the political state of France, and the *existence* of all those who had already declared themselves in favour of the Bourbons.[1] It is to the period of the Empire, therefore, that an effort to present the marvellous Corsican's career with due respect to that *unity* which fits a story for the stage, would best be confined.

Theatrical situations and telling effects are, of course, to be found throughout the life of Napoleon. Splendid opportunities are offered, both in the brilliant years before the Empire and the pathetic days at St. Helena. But it is rather to the historical painter than to the playwright that the dramatic situations during both those periods appeal. The 13th Vendémiaire, the 18th Brumaire, the bridge at Arcole. . . . a score of others, are sore temptations, and to be met only by rigorous adhesion to those inexorable principles of composition which the exigencies of theatrical representation no less than the canons of good taste demand. In any other life any one of such crises must have been seized upon. But in the case of Bonaparte, Fortune has been so prodigal of splendors, that even the breathless interest of the 18th Brumaire, if used, would be an ante-climax.

With his first abdication in April, 1814, the curtain really falls upon Napoleon. The rest is but that natural "ever afterward" to which the skill of the

[1] Memoirs, Vol. III., 435 (Scribner's).

dramatist and the imagination of the audience con-
sign the people in a play when falls the final curtain.

The dazzling return from Elba, the Hundred Days,
Waterloo, the English prison-ship . . . are, it
must be confessed, a costly sacrifice to make upon
the altar of the unities; but made it must be. Indeed, these thrilling scenes form but an episode in
no wise capable of being woven into the finished plot.
They were an unexpected flicker from the socket-
sunk taper of a life. It was as if his audience,
Europe, unwilling or unable to think him gone, had
noisily demanded one more look at the peerless
actor.

The curtain was rung up again. A feverish, unutterable burst of acting follows. But it is the same
last act. Nothing not said and done before is added:
no situation, no *motif* is new. He abdicates once
more. Again the treacheries, the biting of the dust,
the broken heart. Again a prisoner on board a ship
bound for an island. Then forever—curtain.

.   .   .   .   .   .

The play begins at Malmaison, the charming coun-
try-house which Josephine had bought. It is the
spring of 1804. *Napoleon* has been First Consul for
five years. Little by little all power had been entrusted to him. The Republic exists in name alone.
He is France. He has not yet said so. The proper
moment has not yet arrived. It is approaching fast.
And there are enemies. There are the Bourbons,
the exiled King of France. And there are the re-

publicans who have remained true to the Revolution. And there are the nameless fears of *Josephine*, *Napoleon's* wife.

Assassination is in the air, has been attempted even. Rumours of Bourbon boldness upon the near frontiers; and Chouan plotters here in the heart of Paris. On every hand suspicion, jealousy, fear of Napoleon. The time has come to strike. The blow falls by an accident upon the young, romantic, innocent Duc D'Enghien, a Bourbon prince.

Europe is horrified; *Napoleon* called a monster. Something must be done, and done at once. There is only one thing to do. The farce must end. The mask be laid aside, the Consulate become the Empire.

At this point our play begins.

All is uneasiness around *Napoleon*. *Josephine*, "his star," predicts the worst—one of the motives of the tragedy. The brothers of the Consul are divided. Two are away, one in disgrace. *Joseph*, the eldest, witty, subservient, politic, will await events. *Lucien*, republican to the core, breaks away. *Talleyrand* and *Fouché* fence for first influence over the man of fate; but neither publicly commits himself as yet. *Napoleon* is at bay! Public opinion has turned against him now. Even the army has grown restless, anxious. His dearest friends, *Mme. de Rémusat*, *Hortense*, his wife, and *Caulaincourt*, entreat, denounce, and apprehend the worst. His councillors are wary, double-faced.

Shall he proclaim himself the state?

His genius, the terrible hallucination of his life, "*Imperator*," appears. The die is cast. "Vive l'Empereur!" The first scene of the drama has been played.

.   .   .   .   .

The splendid ceremonies of the coronation have at last ended. The members of the Court, fatigued and not too much at home, wander about the galleries of the Tuileries ; gossip and conjecture and jealousy abound.

Napoleon's sister, *Caroline Murat*, begins her work of malice with *Fouché*. The venerable and saintly *Pope, Pius VII.*, now installed in the Pavilion of Flora, is to receive the Court this evening. The Emperor realizes himself superbly. The zenith being now reached, nobody thinks that the decline must of necessity begin—nobody feels this but the Empress : she does intensely. The shadow of the coming fate appears to her, but it is now no larger than a man's hand. Wait !

The Emperor projects his policy. His star is blazing in the blue above. Near the horizon only do we detect how rapidly stars, having once reached the meridian, fall.

The cloud has cast its shadow on the face of the aged Pope. The Emperor's first night is not devoid of dreams, nor are the dreams of glory only. And now more blows, more startling acts, more glory are required.

Three years have passed. The map of Europe has been changed. Its thrones have been at the disposal of *Napoleon.*

Eylau and Friedland have just been added to the bright chaplet of his victories. He has retired to winter quarters at the Castle of Finkenstein. Europe in chorus sings his praises. But the cloud is larger than a man's hand now. *Josephine* at Mayence, lies beneath it, wretched.

Another woman now is in her place. "The only woman that Napoleon ever really loved." A timid and deep-eyed, passionate creature whom accident had brought within the magic reach of the all-powerful man. She now becomes the second motive of the theme—lies like an undefined but irresistible sub-influence in *Napoleon's* heart, is heard like an unspeakably sweet alto to *Josephine's* own plaint— an alto at the last to mingle so sublimely, too, in those pathetic cadences at Malmaison.

She, *Countess Walewska,* here in mid-winter at cold Finkenstein, knows only that she loves *Napoleon,* and that she lies secure, hushed, happy beyond all dreams, within his arms.

Rustan, the Mameluke slave, stirs up the great wood fire. *Napoleon* burns up Josephine's last letter. *Marie Walewska* sings sitting at his feet. The world is at his feet, too—let the cold wind blow to-night. The spring is coming. He will return to France covered with glory. The night has fallen. More wood there, *Rustan!* It is dark.

And this girl at his feet has come to teach him love. Paris is far away—too far to hear the sobs of *Josephine*, who somehow cannot sleep.

. . . . . .

The Conqueror of the World is back in France. *Fête* after *fête* attests the people's joy. There is to be a jolly party of his friends at Fontainebleau. About the grounds groups of friends wander.

Upon the terrace two friends are discovered when the curtain rises on this scene. He does not hear what all these friends have got to say. They come and go in groups of two and three.

There is a little music now : some games, a lame attempt at dancing. Something is wrong. The merrymaking is a lugubrious failure. Will nobody explain? Where's *Talleyrand?* *Fouché*, *Joseph*, *Mme. de Rémusat*, *Mme. Murat?* All dumb as oysters. "Later," whispers the tantalizing *Talleyrand*. The devil! Where's *Josephine?* Ah! here on the terrace! The cloud has hid the sun! Away with it! Nor must our dear *Walewska* remain another moment! *Fouché* must be suppressed! *Mme. Murat*, be patient! All in good season—even your hate shall satiate itself. To-day is *Josephine's* and honour's and the new quadrille's.

. . . . .

Out at Saint-Cloud there is a secret apartment. Two years have passed away. *Josephine's* star has sunk into a sea of troubles. The giant has been forging his resistless way into the very heart of universal power. Five years an Emperor. The world is blind, and wondering, and afraid. There is no limit to this man's dominion! And yet the vast and splendid fabric of his power has no foundation but his own frail life. There is no heir. There is no hope of one. The world cannot contrive to see, with all its spying, so far into *Napoleon's* motives as it would. Its sight cannot by any means reach to the little secret *boudoir* of this scene, nor its alarmed imagination conjure a guess so mad as is the truth.

Marie Walewska, about to be the mother of Napoleon's child, lives in that small apartment at Saint-Cloud.

The graceful *Talleyrand* meets *Fouché's* much less graceful, blunt, "divorce her," by the adroit suggestion that *Josephine* can have a child by proxy and no one be the wiser. And if a child—why not this child? But he does not allow sufficiently for what he probably was not aware existed outside the *bourgeoisie*, namely maternal instincts. At all events, here are a dove, a leopardess, a giant, and a babe entangled in the meshes of his net—and nothing landed. Indeed his cause is lost : not he! He merely leaves the sinking *Josephine*, and gives *Fouché's* less politic designs the needed *savoir-faire*. Divorce it must be. The cloud has covered all the heavens now. The man of Destiny soars not from henceforth ; crashes, the rather, in trackless, lightless space, do-

ing what harm he can—to no one so much harm as
to himself, the Destroyer!

But the tinkling of the lute, and the low plaintive
contralto—heard not beyond the walls of the *boudoir*
—the world of love and of imagination in his *Marie's*
eyes, these still are his—here let him rest in peace a
little while.

. . . .

At terribly historic Fontainebleau there is a gallery with a succession of embrasured windows. In
one of these *Fouché* is to unfold to *Josephine* the now
perfected scheme for the divorce. France is his text.

If it were merely to make room for some fresh
wanton favourite, who would denounce it so inexor-
ably as he, *Fouché?* If it were possible to hope
for a legitimate child! And any other—bah! what
honourable man could dream of so imposing upon
France?

What then? Shall the Imperial power descend to
one or other of the Bonapartes?

It is enough! The victim has been bound by
cords the strength of which *Fouché* knew well
enough. The sacrifice is the supremest in history—
it means a living agony of death—but it is for him,
Napoleon; it is for France! Come in, thou man of
Fate—thy evening hastens, but now the fires of this
thy evening sacrifice shall light the moments which
remain for thee: Come in, and show thy wife thy
Policy. She is thy star. She will not fail thee now.

At Malmaison again after five years. A woman lies there dying—it is she, *Josephine*, the outcast Empress of the French.

Death has no terrors, but this bad news is quite too hard to bear. He is in trouble; *Napoleon* has been trampled to the earth.

Here by her, is *Hortense*, herself a Queen—more than outcast. And here, miraculously so, is she who reigned supreme over the man who ruled the world—*Marie Walewska!*

She and her boy, who also is Napoleon's, and by the bed of *Josephine*, who lies here dying—dying and wishing that she could help *Napoleon!*

The pleasure palace, this of Malmaison, witnesses much these days.

And death and *Napoleon's* ruin come nearer day by day. The Star has set forever—and he knows it.

Through the long watches of those awful nights these three think of him, speak of him, pray for him, ceaselessly. These three. And he remembers —now that he cannot hope.

.   .   .

It is not far from Malmaison to Fontainebleau: and it is here at Fontainebleau that the ruined man has at last fallen. Few remain faithful. On these he throws himself in hopeless, helpless pleadings. In vain. At every point, in very love, they have to show him that nothing now can possibly be done.

He abdicates—withdraws his abdication—appeals

once more. Offers unheard-of victories to France—anything.

The Marshals come back to him hopeless. Absolute abdication. His son—for whom he flung away his Star—must be involved in his own ruin. Fate is ironical.

And *Josephine* is dying as he frets, and fumes, and gnaws his heart away.

Death! Let death end all. But even death had sided with the Bourbons, it would not come to him, although he conjured it with deadly drugs.

No, he must live to drink the dregs of grief and desolation and remorse.

Darkness is falling on those two royal palaces. In one *Hortense* is kissing her dead mother's face; and in the other, at midnight, even *Rustan* the black slave, slinks from his post outside *Napoleon's* door and flees, thus leaving him alone with memory.

CURTAIN.

BRIEF PERSONAL OUTLINES.

NAPOLEON.

The appearance and general characteristics of the First Napoleon are too familiar to call for any lengthy notice here. The gossip of his secretaries, valets, and close friends has supplied us with a few of his habitual traits, tricks, and moods, which may be used by the player to the heightening of the colour of his portrayal.

Private Secretary *Bourrienne* speaks of Napoleon's wont to sit on tables rather than chairs when interested or excited ; his jerky, mussy way of taking snuff (to which *Las Cases* demurs, loyally denying excess in its use, etc.) ; and his absent-minded moods, during which he would countermand every command, and keep his servants and *aides* running about to no purpose. *Mme. de Rémusat* describes his dress, in which he exercised a studied negligence —while tyrannically punctilious as to the appearance of everyone else.

Another Secretary, *Meneval*, tells of his superstitious moods, and the supernatural effect upon him of church bells. *Las Cases* records his habit of crossing himself perpetually. *Chancellor Pasquier* testifies to Napoleon's great tenderness in times of sorrow, or quiet joy.

Lucien Bonaparte.

"Tall, ill-shaped . . . very near-sighted," says the chatty *Mme. Junot* (*Duchess of Abrantès*), of Lucien. He "had a fiery soul," according to *Pasquier;* was the bitterest enemy of Josephine, complains the gallant *Bourrienne:* most independent and quick-tempered, declares *Mme. Junot.*

Joseph Bonaparte.

Brother Joseph was "witty, voluptuous, and effeminate," if *Pasquier* does him justice. He had, none the less, "a handsome face," was "fond of the society of women," and was possessed of "gentler manners than any of his brothers," says *Mme. de Rémusat.*

Talleyrand.

Talleyrand was polished to a degree, a survival, in manners, of the *old régime*, and the typical master of ceremonies—all in addition to a depth and duplicity of heart and mind never surpassed. (*Thiers.*) He "was careful in his dress, used perfumes, and was a lover of good cheer and all the pleasures of the senses," according to *Mme. de Rémusat.*

Fouché.

"Careless of his appearance, he wore the gold lace and ribbons which were the insignia of his dignities as if he disdained to arrange them . . . . active, animated, always restless." So far *Mme. de Rémusat.* He maintained always, says *Pasquier*, "the outward appearance of imperturbable coolness." Indifference, perfidy, and cunning are generally accorded to him.

Pius VII.

At the time he was about sixty-two years old ; but his appearance and bearing were most venerable. *Saint-Amand* speaks of the transparent holiness of the old man which commanded the reverent homage of the very atheists of Paris. "I never saw a man with a finer countenance," exclaims Rapp. (*Bourrienne.*)

CAULAINCOURT.

He had, says the *Duchess of Abrantès*, "as much the manners of a gentleman as any man in France ;" and his "air of reserve," the Duchess thinks, only "superficial persons took for haughtiness."

NEY.

Napoleon's snappish charge that Marshal Ney was "factious," is due to Ney's unfailing firmness and frankness. He was a blunt, out-spoken, soldierly man. (*Thiers, Scott, Bourrienne.*)

MACDONALD.

This Marshal was a man of very quiet but tremendous firmness of manner ; less blunt, but quite as positive as Ney. (*Bourrienne.*)

CONSTANT.

The valet of Napoleon for many years, from whose *Memoirs* we learn of the hero in dishabille. *Constant* was a dry wit and a kindly man withal.

YVAN.

Was the Court Physician who was in attendance at Fontainebleau on the night of the Emperor's attempt at suicide. (*Hazlitt.*)

RUSTAN.

This man was a Mameluke slave given to Napoleon in Egypt, in 1798, by the Sheik El Bekri, on the occasion of a festival. He became attached to Napoleon's person, sleeping at his door, and jealously guarding it. Like his race, he was silent, oracular, and possessed of the loyal courage of a blood-hound. (*Bourrienne.*)

CARDINAL FESCH.

A maternal uncle to Napoleon, who with considerable courage sided with the Church against the Emperor. Dignified. (*Bourrienne.*)

IMPERATOR.

I have ventured to embody in a bodiless ghost those hallucinations to which Napoleon was subject, and which most frequently emanated from his absorbing thoughts on Charlemagne.

JOSEPHINE.

It were impertinent to sketch in a few lines so well-known a personage. It may be well for the actress to remember, however, that in every situation (even the death-bed scene), the charming Empress was conscious of the fact that "appearances are worth while," and that the minutest point of toilet and adornment is worthy of attention. For details consult the *Memoirs* of *Mlle. Avrillion.*

COUNTESS WALEWSKA.

Of this woman, "the only one Napoleon ever really loved," *Saint-Amand* says that she was a "charming person, with light hair, blue eyes, a brilliant complexion, a graceful figure, and dignified carriage." All writers mention her melancholy sweetness, which "only added to her beauty."

HORTENSE.

The unfortunate daughter of Josephine had become, by the time of our play, broken and ill. Dignity, reserve, and earnestness, would seem to have been her strongest traits. (*Mme. de Rémusat, Mme. Junot, Saint-Amand.*)

MME. DE RÉMUSAT.

To the graceful pen of *M. de Talleyrand* we owe our exact knowledge of the charms of *Mme. de Rémusat's* personality. (See his letter of 29th April, 1811.)

From scores of adjectives take these : "Graceful, unaffected, not thin, mingled tenderness and vivacity." It seems that she was given to wearing her hair over her forehead (bangs?)—"and that," says the former Bishop of Autun, "is a pity."

MME. MURAT.

"Struck me as very charming," generously exclaims her contemporary at Court, *Mme. de Rémusat.* (*Memoirs.*) "She bore a great resemblance to the Emperor," and was possessed of "seductive charms," says *Pasquier.* (*Memoirs.*)

BABETTE.

As to the fair *Babette*, we trust there is no reason why she *might* not have been historical.

ACT I.

AT BAY.—1804.

ACT I.

Scene 1.--- *The Library at Malmaison.*[1]

Discovered—Joseph *and* Lucien Bonaparte *angrily discussing. A large table strewn with maps and papers; chairs, desks, globes, etc., etc.*

Joseph.

Fudge! Bah! Absurd! Lucien, you are a fool!—fool!

Lucien.

Coward! You are not! Joseph, you are a tool!

Joseph.

A tool? In whose hands, pray? Not in Napoleon's?

Lucien.

Yes!

Joseph.

No.

Lucien.

I say yes!

Joseph.

No!

Lucien.

      I say you lie, then !
I say that you are privy to his foul schemes.
I say you've set a price upon your honour.
You are infected with his base ambition.
He has deceived the world and you completely.
And who can wonder at it ? Look at these lines !
    (*Picks up a map of Europe from the table.*)
Here, these red, braggart, pencilled lines—look at
  them !
Then look at this ! This was the France of Nature
Until the bloody finger of his rashness
Smeared France, France, France, on lands that are
  not France. Look !
And the end is not yet. No ! You hope to see
The whole of Europe forced into France by blood.

Joseph.

You missed your calling, Lucien, by my soul, man !
You should have gone into the Church. Ha, ha, ha !

Lucien.

Perhaps ! Pretend I am a priest already,
Come now, confess to me. Have you not plotted
Murder?

    Joseph.

  Murder, you say ?

Lucien.

Of the Republic.

Joseph.

Oh! of the Republic! I thought you might mean
Of the Duc d'Enghien. You start! You did not
    know!

Lucien.

You cannot mean it. Napoleon is not mad?
His butchery of armies men can forgive;
He knows how to transmute gore into glory.
But let him know that when he adds the murder
Of a Bourbon to his crimes, Europe will rise!

Joseph.

You think so? Not so bad as that? Might lose
    friends.

Lucien.

If you have influence with him, warn him now.
But then, you cannot mean it, Joseph. Tell me!

Joseph.

I will! But—ha! ha! ha! ha! ha! ha! ha! ha!
Lucien, you do remind me of a story.
Sit down, man, while I tell it—it is so good!
There was a cobbler once who had a wife, and—

Lucien.

This man would tipple at his own funeral!

Joseph.

And fourteen children living, and more in view—

Lucien.

Damn everyone of them at once! Now tell me.
What is this matter of the Duc d'Enghien?
Napoleon did not eat, nor sleep, nor quarrel![2]
Something is all wrong. Madame de Rémusat
Looked like a ghost.[3] Josephine sighed and sim-
    pered.[4]
Couriers kept coming with their infernal racket.
I could not sleep nor ascertain the nature
Of all this mystery.[5] Come, now, what is it?
Another *coup d'état?* What *is* my brother?
King? Emperor? Czar? or is he great Mogul?

Joseph.

Not yet! Not yet! But when he is, remember
He may remember these indiscretions, boy!

Lucien.

Let him remember! Let him remember more!
Let him remember who helped him in Brumaire;[6]
Whose voice it was upheld him in the Tribune;
Who seconded his measures against all odds;
Who silenced all his foes in the Five Hundred;
Let him remember that it was Lucien. I,[7]
I who would gladly die for the Republic!
Let him remember furthermore, that Lucien

Did not forsake him 'till he forsook old France ;
But that, when he unmasked himself a tyrant,
Trampled the liberties of France beneath him,
Outraged the sacred comity of nations,
And for his own advancement forswore all faith,
Broke vows, betrayed old friends, lied—yes! and
  murdered.[8]
  . . . *Then* I denounced him! Let him remem-
  ber that!

Joseph.

Wh—ew! Lucien, what in the devil's name, means
  this?
Who has been stirring up all your bad blood thus?
You really do Napoleon injustice.
His very life is not safe now in Paris.
It is all honeycombed with Chouan plotters,[9]
In close communication with the Bourbons.
Napoleon really must defend himself.[10]

Lucien.

Has he no friends?

Joseph.

No! he has only courtiers.[11]

Lucien.

True! True! Napoleon now must protect himself.
Had he been true—but never mind! What about
D'Enghien? Has he been apprehended—murdered?

Joseph.

Arrested, but on Napoleon's word, quite safe.

Lucien.

God grant it, but I have my doubts. Where is he?

Joseph.

At Vincennes.[12]

Lucien.

So near as that? I fear some wrong.
If—but why anticipate? Where is Fouché?

Joseph.

Here.

Lucien.

And Talleyrand?

Joseph.

Here too.

Lucien.

And Caulaincourt?

Joseph.

Not yet returned. But why?

Lucien.

I wish he had, then.

Joseph.

You puzzle me.

Lucien.

Pray, do not alarm yourself,
For I meant nothing by it.   I do not like
Fouché, nor Talleyrand, you know.   I do like
Caulaincourt, and I regret his being sent
On any such nefarious expedition.[13]

Joseph.

It is extremely close here.   Let us go out.

Lucien.

In heaven's name, Joseph,—out on the terrace.
Something is choking me—like D'Enghien's fingers.

Joseph.

Nonsense! Come! Depend upon Napoleon's word.
Come! Come! France is Napoleon.   Don't be ab-
    surd.   (*Exeunt.*

Enter MME. DE RÉMUSAT, *hurrying and sobbing.*

Mme. de Rémusat.

Monsieur Lucien! Monsieur Lucien!   Where are
    you?

Re-enter LUCIEN *and* JOSEPH.

Lucien.

Here!   Madame de Rémusat—Crying!   What!
    Speak!

Mme. de Rémusat.

The Duc—the Duc—d'Enghien—was shot this
morning.

Lucien.

Napoleon! Was it for this I bled for you?
Joseph, this means the end! This is perdition!

Joseph.

Fool! Cannot you read the writing on the wall?
It means the Empire—

Lucien.

Hold! Not another word!
Madame, where is my brother? God! What a deed
Is this! No prate of destiny will mend it.

Mme. de Rémusat.

He is with Messieurs Talleyrand and Fouché,
I believe--raves madly over a mistake
Which had been made.[14]

Lucien.

Mistake? Damnable error!

Joseph.

Enough of this. Come! Has Josephine been told?

Mme. de Rémusat.

'Twas she who told me. She's paralyzed with grief;

Moans that her doom is fixed; predicts death, ruin,
Napoleon's overthrow—everything dreadful.[15]

Lucien.

And she is right.

Joseph.

Perhaps she is, fool--idiot!
But my advice is now, that you hold your tongue.
I know Napoleon better than you do, Sir,
He is at bay. Beware! Come, Madame, with me.
(*Exeunt* JOSEPH *and* MME. DE RÉMUSAT.

Lucien.

At bay, is he? Hark! Is that the yelping pack?
(*Clatter of angry voices heard without.*)
(*Exit* LUCIEN, *musing.*

Enter CONSTANT, *the valet.*

Constant.

(*Crossing quickly to* L.)
Dear! dear! *dear! dear!! dear!!!* It is, "Constant, do that!"
I do't, and then it is, "Constant, you blockhead,
What are you doing that for?" T-r-r-r-rumpery!
(*Hurries away to* L.

Enter BABETTE *at* L., *meets* CONSTANT.

Babette.

Babette this! Babette that! Here! There! Everywhere!

Not a solitary wink of sleep all night !
Hyster-r-r-r-r-r-r-rics !
  (*Sails across.*)

Constant.

Citizeness Babette seems much excited ! [16]

Babette.

No, Citizen Constant, I'm not excited.
I'm mad !   Madame called me a little ninny !

Constant.

Is that all ?   Called you a little ninny, eh ?
What's that compared to having a boot-jack thrown
Square at your head ?   Called you a little ninny !
How would you like to have to shave a madman ?
I had to chase him round the room all lathered, [17]
And shave him on the fly, while he was writing,
Talking, tearing, ramping, ordering—stark mad !

Babette.

And what's the matter, eh, Citizen Constant ?

Constant.

What is the matter ?   Oh ! heaven only knows ;
Citizen Talleyrand says one thing ; Fouché
Another.   Between ourselves, Babette, both lie.
They're deep, but not so deep as is their master.
They think they know him through and through—
    They do not.
One has to shave a man before he knows him.

Babette.

And that's true, Citizen Constant, with women.
Would you believe it? Madame dressing and dressed
Is not the same creature—not by any means.

Constant.

Not really? Eh?

Babette.

Upon my word of honour.

Constant.

And what's the main distinction? Of quality?

Babette.

Of quantity, ha, ha, ha, ha, quantity!
The madame the world knows is a composite;
Heaven made a part, and I do all the rest.

Constant.

The finished article does you both credit.

Babette.

(*Courtesying.*)
Heaven thanks Citizen Constant as I do.
But what, since you're so knowing, is in the air?

Constant.

Can you keep secrets?

Babette.

      I keep secrets!   How long
Do you imagine that I would be allowed
To dress and undress Madame, if I could not ?

Constant.

True!   Citizeness Babette—of course, of course.
Well then, I'll tell you.   What's in the air, you say ?
This, dear Babette ; there's going to be a change.

Babette.

What !   You're not going without informing me ?

Constant.

 (*Returning.*)
Promise not to tell !

Babette.

     Quick !   Someone is calling !
(*Voices heard without.*)

Constant.

Citizeness Babette, my master is deep !
Ha, ha, ha, ha, ha !   Adieu, my dear Babette.
            (*Exit.*

Babette.

Preposterous man ! preposterous monster !
Are they all gone daft ?   And over what, forsooth ?
So far as I can see they have done nothing

But kill one Bourbon! That's nothing new in
> France.

There's something in this! Mark my words! *I'll*
> find out!

I'll dr-r-r-ress it out of Madame before dinner!

(*Exit.*

(NAPOLEON'S *voice heard without.*)

Enter NAPOLEON *and* JOSEPHINE *who clings to him.*[18]

Josephine.

Bonaparte, don't be a King, I beg of you!
Am I not Josephine, your star?—You said so.[19]

Napoleon.

I thought that Lucien was here, and Joseph. Don't,
Don't, Josephine—this is no time for weakness.[20]
> (*Disengages himself.*)

Somebody, there! Command my brother's pres-
> ence.

Now, wife, what is it? Crying! Fie, Josephine!
I shall be forced to add the name of D'Enghien
To the long list of those of whom I have been
Jealous, if you so mourn him.[21] Come, come, my
> star,

The crisis of my fortune has been reached. This
> day,

This day I am to fight the battle of my life!
And you desert me? It is not kind of you.

Josephine.

But was it necessary to destroy him ?

Napoleon.

As the event proved, yes. There was some errour.[22]
My orders were not followed.   I cannot say
Who dared to disobey me till Caulaincourt
Arrives.   But then, this is not women's business![23]
Josephine, look you.   The trouble of your dreams
Last night .   .   .   [24]

Josephine.

Last night?   Say for a year, Napoleon.

Napoleon.

The trouble of your dreams had a foundation.

Josephine.

Alas ! Napoleon, the troubled dreams of wives
Are never causeless.   The shadows which events
Are said to cast as they approach, fall always
First upon the white solicitude which makes
So large a portion of every true wife's life—
Solicitude so white, so sensitive, that
Any shadow, aye, be it no larger than
A man's hand even, is ominous enough
To terrify, to break one's heart, as mine breaks.

Napoleon.

Don't, Josephine, don't! You know I can't bear
this!
Come, sit down, darling. I have much to say to
you.

Josephine.

Say anything, but . . .

Napoleon.

But what?

Josephine.

You know but what.

Napoleon.

Well then, I will not. But you must hear me out.
(JOSEPHINE *sits;* NAPOLEON *walks about.*)
My star rose at Arcola.[25] Before that day
Power was a pastime and Destiny a word.
The victories which crowned my arms on all sides
Meant scarcely more to me than the caresses
Of that mistress, Fate, who would grow tired of me
And leave me in the lurch at some great crisis.
The flatteries of France intoxicated,
But did not deceive me. I was not so young
As to imagine that men really loved me.
They feared me. I knew that. But let me lose
one
Battle, and I could hear their sneers of "Upstart!"

Yes! Scores of times, in dreams upon my camp-
    bed
I have lost that fight, and France has spit at me.[26]
But, Josephine, at Arcola, I saw it.
When I had worked that miracle, Destiny
Blazed, and for the first time, I beheld myself.
That night I saw it. Are you prepared to hear?
I saw the shade of Charlemagne, Josephine!
Crowned, bearing the conquered world in his right
    hand.
He beckoned to me. And I came back to France
An Emperor!

               Josephine.

    No!

               Napoleon.

          Yes! Josephine, in soul!
An Emperor, in my imagination.
Imagination rules the world.[27] And I shall!
From thenceforth all was changed. The map of
    Europe,
The boundaries of nations, the thrones of kings—
All was to be at my disposal. What, then,
Was the poltroon Directory, what all France,
That they should give *me* orders, hamper *my* will?
The Eighteenth Brumaire was a necessity.
I must become First Consul, or all was lost.

               Josephine.

You are First Consul, Bonaparte. Now, what more?

Napoleon.

This, Josephine. Look at the map of Europe.
These red lines show what has been done already.
All they include is France, or subject to her;
But nothing is secure. At any moment
What may this multiplicity of counsels [38]
Not undo? An Empire needs an Emperor:
France is an Empire, and Destiny calls me!

Josephine.

Pause, Bonaparte. I also have seen visions.
I've seen Death sitting upon the throne of France.

Enter a Servant.

Napoleon.

It is time, then, that I dethrone Death. Well?
Well?

Servant.

Citizen General Caulaincourt.

Napoleon.

Admit him!
Now, Josephine, for heaven's sake be quiet.

Josephine.

Yes! Yes!

Enter CAULAINCOURT *and* HORTENSE.

That murderer, Hortense! Avoid him! [39]

Napoleon.

Hold your tongue, madame! Well, Caulaincourt,
  explain!

Hortense.

He will! He will! He has explained already.

Napoleon.

Hush, Hortense! Who disobeyed me, Caulaincourt?

Caulaincourt.

General, not I. I was obedient.[30]

Napoleon.

As ever, Caulaincourt. But of my letter?[31]
I wrote them to postpone the execution.
Savary says that no such letter reached him.
Oh! if it had, all this might have been spared us.

Josephine.

And you are innocent of D'Enghien's blood?[32]

Napoleon.

Am I not, Caulaincourt?

Caulaincourt.

                    Alas! I fear not!

Napoleon.

How! Traitor! Scoundrel! You turn upon me, too?

Caulaincourt.

The Citizen First Consul has a few friends——

Napoleon.

Has he, indeed? Thanks! He can dispense with you.

Josephine.

Must General Caulaincourt insult his chief
When all the world seems to be turned against him?

Caulaincourt.

Madame did not observe that the First Consul
Would not allow me to conclude my sentence.

Napoleon.

Pardon me, pray. There were some other insults?

Caulaincourt.

With the First Consul's pardon, I meant to say,
That the First Consul has yet a few true friends
Who tell him the plain truth. I am one of them.[33]

Napoleon.

And the plain truth is——

Caulaincourt.

       That the First Consul wished
The execution of the Duc d'Enghien!

Napoleon.

I ordered it postponed!

Caulaincourt.

                    Postponed—in order
To extort important secrets from him first.[34]
But let none of the guilt be the First Consul's :
Let me be punished.   I was not near Vincennes,
Nor had I heard about the horrid murder
Until I came here.   I obeyed my orders.
I was commanded to arrest D'Enghien.
I did arrest him ; brought him to Savary.
I disapproved this, but did not disobey.[35]
Therefore I, Caulaincourt, must be called butcher.
Did I not seize him? bring him to the shambles?
The innocence of the First Consul is quite clear.[36]
Madame is right.   Yes, I am the murderer.
Of the First Consul I have no more to ask
Than that he may remember that it was through
Unquestioning obedience that Caulaincourt
Came to disgrace.   My sword.   Mesdames, my
    homage.
        (*Offers his sword to* NAPOLEON.)

                    Napoleon.
Keep it ; but go !
                        (*Exit* CAULAINCOURT.
                    I shall need swords like that one.
Hortense, you saved him. Had it not been for you,
I should have flung him from me, as I have scores.

                    Hortense.
Grant me another boon, and I'll believe you.

Josephine.

Hortense, implore him, to resist temptation.

Enter Mme. Murat, *unobserved.*

Napoleon.

You are not discreet. Hortense herself, my dear,
Is a temptation!

Mme. Murat.

(*Aside.*)   Did I not know as much?

Hortense.

(*Kneeling.*)
Succumb to me then!

Mme. Murat.

(*Aside.*)   Dear me! before his wife!

Hortense.

Succumb!

Napoleon.

I do. What is your pleasure, Hortense?

Hortense.

That you will not be hoodwinked by Mme. Murat.⁵⁷

Mme. Murat.

(*Aside.*)
Indeed! I like that.

Josephine.

     Pray, Hortense, be cautious!

Mme. Murat.

(*Aside.*)
These Beauharnais!

Napoleon.

     Is Caroline still plotting?

Hortense.

Ceaselessly, fiendishly, against my mother.[38]

Josephine.

Hortense!

Napoleon.

     Bourrienne! Constant! There, somebody!

           Enter CONSTANT.

Call Madame Murat!

                   (*Exit* CONSTANT.

Mme. Murat.

     Madame Murat is here!

Napoleon.

Josephine, Hortense, leave her alone with me.

           (*Exeunt* JOSEPHINE *and* HORTENSE.

Well, vixen, marplot, what are you hatching now?

Mme. Murat.

Ha, ha, ha, ha, ha, ha, ha, ha, ha, ha! ha!

Napoleon.

You have been nosing with Citizen Fouché.

Mme. Murat.

Yes, we've been nosing, and we have smelt a rat.

Napoleon.

We know too much of one another, sister,
For this tomfoolery.   What are you up to?

Mme. Murat.

Trying to save you—but, then, what is the use?
Don't be a fool, Napoleon!   These Beauharnais
Stand between you and glory, and while you waste
These precious hours in mooning with an idiot
Whom you call your wife——

Napoleon.

      By the cross, Caroline!

Mme. Murat.

Yes! and in fondling that little chit, Hortense,
Whom all the world believes to be your mistress,[39]
The opportunity of all your life slips
Through your foolish fingers.[40] Have you no courage?
Europe is hissing you: France calling you names.
Paris is all aflame: the army restless.
And resignations by the score are threatened.
Why, Bonaparte, your very servants giggle,
And all the household feels that your end has come.

Napoleon.

In God's name, then, I'll show them what end has
    come.   (*Exit Napoleon.*

Mme. Murat.

These are the moments which make up history !

Enter RUSTAN.

Rustan, the Citizen Fouché is somewhere.
Give him the compliments of Madame Murat,
And this.   (*Writes a brief note.*)
            So ! Lose no time. You understand me ?

Rustan.

To hear is to obey.
    (*Starts toward the door.*)

Mme. Murat.

           And return quickly.
And then remain near the First Consul's person,
Prepared for anything.   He is in danger.

Rustan.

Rustan will be prepared. Rustan is sleepless.
            (*Exit, fingering his poniard.*

Mme. Murat.

God ! If I only were a man, I'd show them !

Enter Fouché.

Fouché.

Madame Murat is not a politician.

Mme. Murat.

By politician you mean coward, doubtless.

Fouché.

Ah! well! But I must beg Madame not to write
Firebrand words like these, to *me*, at any rate.

Mme. Murat.

The Citizen Fouché has changed his mind, then?

Fouché.

Say his words, rather. His mind remains un-
changed.[11]
Citizen Talleyrand has undertaken
To advocate my dangerous policy,
Which is extremely good of him. It leaves me
Free to oppose my policy in public.
Which I shall do, as every passing hour
Deepens the danger which surrounds the Consul.
And Talleyrand is very near a statesman:[42]
He lies so well, and nobody expects him
To mean a word he says; but Fouché is good!
The Chaplain of all the immoralities[43]
Cannot impair his reputation, can he?
No, Talleyrand must act: Fouché be silent.

Enter NAPOLEON, TALLEYRAND, JOSEPH, and LUCIEN.

Talleyrand.

When the First Consul asks whence came my for-
    tune,
I merely answer that I bought stock in France
The day before the Eighteenth Brumaire, and sold
On the day after. The profit realized
Was the foundation of my fortune.[44]

Lucien.

(*Aside.*)   Hear him!

Napoleon.

Citizen Talleyrand has told the truth there.

Fouché.

And yet how gracefully withal! It sounded
Quite as smooth as any lie I ever heard!

Napoleon.

You jest, Fouché? This is no time for jesting.
God's wounds! Am I a dog for you to harry?
Joseph, since you alone seem to be a man,
Tell them what my determination is. Speak!

Lucien.

Think twice before you do so! I beseech you!

Napoleon.

Lucien, I have endured enough from you. Speak!
    (*To* JOSEPH.)

Fouché.

Were it not best that such a proclamation
Should emanate from the established—

Napoleon.

(*To* JOSEPH.)   Speak!

Talleyrand.

Best wait until we feel the pulse of Europe.

Fouché.

And of the army.   Savary fears the worst.

Lucien.

And the resignation of Chateaubriand [5]
Has just arrived: does that mean nothing, think
    you?

Joseph.

Truly, Napoleon, there does seem need of care.

Napoleon.

Out!   Malediction!   Have I no friends?   Rustan!

Enter RUSTAN *brandishing his poniard.*

Rustan.

Rustan sleeps not.   In which heart first?

Napoleon.

                            Hold, hell-dog!
Find Madame Bonaparte, and bid her come here.

Talleyrand.

Are we to understand that even our lives
Are jeopardized in the First Consul's presence ?

Napoleon.

No, Talleyrand, no !   Withdraw that calumny !

Talleyrand.

I do.   Before Madame arrives, however,
Permit me to withdraw.   My veneration
For her is so deep, that I cannot consent
To have her witness what, I am now convinced,
It will become my very painful duty
Both to say and do.

Mme. Murat.

    (*Aside to* Lucien.)
           Do you hear that, Lucien ?
I had not heard of this amour ; had you ?

Napoleon.

Go, Talleyrand, by all means, but be assured
That you shall not escape, if harm befall me,
Nor profit by my favour, if I succeed.
Sycophant, coward, sneak, I shall unveil you !

       Enter Josephine, *slowly.*

Talleyrand.

When the First Consul requires my services—

Napoleon.

I shall know, Talleyrand, just what to expect.
You are a thief, a coward without honour.[46]
You don't believe in God, whose priest you once
    were.
You've been a traitor all your life to duty.
Nothing is sacred to you. You would sell God !
Have I not loaded you with gifts, you ingrate ?
Yet there is nothing that you would hesitate
To do against me, if I should be in straits.
You wish me to proclaim myself Emperor,
But don't dare to publicly commit yourself
Until the risk be past, and this unhappy
Matter of D'Enghien blown over. Hypocrite !
Who drove me to deal cruelly with him? You![47]
By whom was I advised of his location ?
You, you, you! I say. What are you scheming for ?
Bah ! I could smash you as I could a wine-glass ;
But I would not touch you. I despise you ! Go !
       (*Exit* TALLEYRAND, *with great dignity.*

Josephine.

My presence was required by the First Consul?

Napoleon.

Ah, Josephine, thrice welcome. I am alone.[48]

Lucien.

There are three Bonapartes at least, Napoleon,
In the First Consul's presence at this moment.

Napoleon.

They do not signify.   Josephine, come here.

Joseph.

By heaven, this is too much.   Come, Caroline.
                    (*Exeunt* JOSEPH *and* CAROLINE.

Josephine.

Don't let them go in anger.   Pray call them back.

Napoleon.

They will return in time : Joseph to borrow,
And Caroline to plot.   Lucien, you still here ?

Lucien.

I am still here, Napoleon, but——

Napoleon.
            Well, Lucien,
Have you read carefully my proposition ?

Lucien.

I have.

Napoleon.
        And ?

Lucien.
            I reject it, and defy you !

Napoleon.

Lucien, I am the man of Destiny, I !
Brother, I beg you in God's name, rise with me.

I am about to found a vast new empire.
Choose any portion of it : it shall be yours.⁴⁹

Fouché.

Provided always that our vast schemes succeed !

Lucien.

You tempt in vain.　You are the blinded victim
Of hallucination—

Josephine.
Have I not said so ?

Lucien.

You ask me to disown my wife in order
That I may the better serve your purposes.
You ask me to believe that you will trample
The powers of Europe underneath your feet ;
That you will soon be able to cut the world
Into as many slices as you have friends.
You are about to murder the Republic.
You will ascend the imperial throne over
The murdered institutions of your country.
Raised up by violence you will require crime
To carry on your universal outrage.
And you will fall—you—and be crushed like this ! ⁵⁰
　　(Seizes a small screen and dashes to pieces.)
　　　　　　　　　　　　　　　　(Exit.

Fouché.

Was he the seventh son ? Saints ! What a preacher !
　　*(Napoleon remains silent a long while and then,
　　　starting up, rushes to the door.)*

Napoleon.

Lucien !　Lucien !—

　　　　　But never mind !

　　　　　　　　　Josephine !

Josephine.

Decide ! decide !—I—

　　　　　This terrible suspense !

Napoleon.

Help me to decide.　I falter, Josephine !

Fouché.

(*Imperator glides in as* FOUCHÉ *speaks.*)
You are in doubt ?　Give France the benefit !

Napoleon.

　　　　　　　　　Go !

　　　　　(*Exit* FOUCHÉ.

Look, Josephine, look !　Charlemagne walks again !

Josephine.

I can see nothing.　You are worn out and dream.
　(NAPOLEON *follows* IMPERATOR, *who lifts the world
　　high in the air.*)

Napoleon.

I will !　I will !—Gone ?

　　　　　　　(*Exit* IMPERATOR.
　　　　　Josephine, the Empire !

CURTAIN.

Scene 2.—*A stately room in the Pavilion of Flora in the palace of the Tuileries. Evening.*[51]

Discovered—Cardinal Fesch *walking with the* Pope. *A throne for* Napoleon; *a smaller throne for His Holiness.*

Fesch.

Your Holiness takes it too seriously.
Did not your Holiness observe, that when His
Imperial Majesty reached forth to take[52]
The Crown, which it had been more seemly he
  should
Have waited to receive, he was excited,
Nervous? It chanced that whence I stood I could
  see
Plainly that His Imperial Majesty,
My nephew, was visibly wrought up and moved.

Pius VII.

Your Eminence had the advantage of us ;
For where we stood—immediately in front,
And near enough to touch—we saw too plainly.
We saw that we had been inveigled into
Our most unusual departure from the
Eternal City by the false promises
Of an ambitious enemy of Holy
Church. We saw that what was heralded abroad·
As the revival of a prerogative,
Now many years denied the Sovereign Pontiffs,

Namely, the right to crown all Christian rulers,[53]
Was made but the occasion of fresh insults.
The upstart crowned himself, while we stood sheep-
    ish,
As though we had incurred the dangers of the
Journey, endured the unaccustomed hardships,
Gone counter to the dictates of our prudence,[54]
Imperilling the person of Christ's Vicar,
And all, forsooth, that we might be made sport of.

Fesch.

It was, indeed, a serious miscarriage;
But I am sure that accident, not malice,
Is to be charged with it. Your Holiness is
In all other points assured of the devout
And filial feelings of His Majesty?

Pius VII.

Yes, they have made an old man comfortable.
More, they have spared no words, no protestations.
I would that we might comfort our poor daughter,
This Josephine, now crowned, when the black tem-
    pest,
Which must inevitably whelm her, comes.
Saw you, my son, from where you stood, Joseph-
    ine's [55]
Face, the moment that the Crown was placed
Upon Napoleon's head? The light of hope went out.
The light burst forth an instant when he crowned
    her,[56]

But it was gone at once, and gone forever!
The surest oracles of prophecy are
Anxious women's eyes, and they're infallible.
Imperial Majesty, beware! beware!
Your arm, my son.   We wish to rest a while.
                    (*Exeunt* PIUS VII. *and* FESCH.

Enter MME. DE RÉMUSAT.

Mme. de Rémusat.

His Holiness not here :   How can I reach him ?

Enter FOUCHÉ.

Ah, Monsieur Fouché.

Fouché.
                    Madame de Rémusat !

Mme. de Rémusat.

Monsieur Fouché will help me?   His Holiness—
Where could I find him?   I thought that he was
    here.
                    Fouché.
His Holiness receives the Court here shortly.

Mme. de Rémusat.

But before that, Monsieur?   It is important.

Fouché.
Doubtless a note would reach him—

Mme. de Rémusat.

Monsieur Fouché!

But how to send it?

Fouché.

If Madame honours me!
(*Voices are heard.*)

Mme. de Rémusat.

Then, Monsieur, at once—and not a word!
(*Gives* Fouché *a note.*)

Fouché.

Trust me!
(*Exit* Mme. de Rémusat.
(*Reads.*)
"The Holy Father: For his own Hands only."
Indeed? And from the Empress! As Minister
Of the Imperial Police and an old
Friend, I must see to it that no curious
Eyes pry into this!
(*Opens the note and goes toward the door.*)
What's this? What's this? What's this?
(*Exit hurriedly.*

Enter M. de Talleyrand, *musing.*

Talleyrand.

H—m! The servant of the servants of the Lord! [57]
He is well housed. If one could manage to get
Into the service of *his* servant's servant,

What else could one desire? I was a Bishop [58]
Once myself! I know just how the hirelings fare.
But this old man seems most miraculously
To have somehow caught reflections of the truth,
And, notwithstanding that he is a Christian,
Contrives in spite of all to remain honest!

Enter Fouché.

Fouché.

Monsieur de Talleyrand!

Talleyrand.

Yours, Monsieur Fouché!
(*They exchange snuff-boxes and pass.*)

Fouché.

(*At the door.*)
Monsieur de Talleyrand!

Talleyrand.

(*Turning at door.*)   Yours, Monsieur Fouché!

Fouché.

There will be music—His Holiness is mad.

Talleyrand.

Monsieur Fouché is thoughtful. He understands
How much I enjoy these Christian harmonies.
I shall come early.

Fouché.

Do! The Coronation
Is the cantata that will be sung to-night.

(*Exeunt.*

Enter Mme. Murat *and* Joseph Bonaparte.

Mme. Murat.

Do you not see that she is playing with us?
And that she has Napoleon under her thumb?
Such airs! Stars! Pauline and I were bound that we
Would drop her train right in the middle of the
Coronation, and we did ; and how she scowled![59]
And then Napoleon stormed at us so, right there,
In Notre Dame, that we picked up the nasty
Train again, to hide our blushes. I tell you,
Joseph, this Beauharnais must be got rid of,
If any of Napoleon's flesh and blood hope
To get on in this world. And let me tell you,
The Faculty of Paris has just declared
That Josephine can never be a mother.

Joseph.

Don't look so devilish, Caroline! Suppose
That Josephine can never be a mother,
Though, with all due respect, I have my own doubts
I cannot, for the life of me, imagine
Just why the Faculty and you should chuckle!

Mme. Murat.

Joseph, you are no politician. Look you!

Napoleon must have somebody, I fancy,
To whom to leave his crown.

Joseph.

All that is settled.

Mme. Murat.

Oh, yes, I know. But how? Why, you yourself have
Told me, that all this talk about your children,
And Louis's, succeeding him, is balderdash.[0]
No! No! There will be no more coronations
In our family, Joseph, unless an heir
Direct turns up.

Joseph.

And this the Faculty and
All of you gossips have formally declared
To be highly improbable?

Mme. Murat.

Impossible!

Joseph.

Worse yet! Well, then, have you as yet decided

Enter Fouché, *quietly.*

What you propose to do?

Mme. Murat.

Divorce Josephine!

Fouché.

Treason, so soon?

Joseph.

No, Monsieur Fouché, gossip!

Fouché.

There is no difference between them, except
That treason is sometimes merciful to souls.

Joseph.

Whereas—

Mme. Murat.

Whereas! Whereas! Don't listen to him!

Joseph.

I leave you, then, Madame. Ha! ha! I pity
You, Monsieur. (*Exit.*

Fouché.

(*Eagerly.*)
Read this and tell me what you think.

Mme. Murat.

What is it?

Fouché.

Read it! Read it!

Mme. Murat.

From Josephine?

Fouché.

Aye, from the Empress and to His Holiness.

Mme. Murat.

How came you by it?

Fouché.

All sorts of offices
Are being created.   They have appointed me
The Grand High Secret Bearer of billets-doux!

Mme. Murat.

By whom appointed?

Fouché.

Madame de Rémusat!

Mme. Murat.

She gave you this?

Fouché.

Implored me to convey it.

Mme. Murat.

She is a bigger fool than I supposed her.

Fouché.

But what a kind fool! Read the note, and say so.

Mme. Murat.

(*Reads the note.*)
" The Empress humbly implores His Holiness
To graciously elucidate a weighty
Matter which much disturbs her.   The Emperor

Has been advised, by some malicious person,
That, as the parish priest was absent from our [61]
Marriage, according to the laws of Holy
Church, no less than those of France, the lawfulness
Of the said marriage might be called in question."

   .   .   .   .   .   .

Monsieur Fouché! If this be true, we—

Fouché.

Read on!

Mme. Murat.

"The eagerness and the great firmness with which
Your Holiness insisted that our marriage
Must take place before Your Holiness would deign
To countenance and bless our coronation." [62]

   .   .   .   .   .

What's this, Monsieur Fouché?　　When was she
    married?

Fouché.

Last night! [63]

Mme. Murat.

And where, pray?

Fouché.

Here, in the Tuileries!

Mme. Murat.

By whom, in heaven's name?

Fouché.

By Cardinal Fesch!

But read, read, read!

Mme. Murat.

   Is she not deep! Where was I?
 (*Reads again.*)
" The eagerness and the great firmness with which
Your Holiness insisted that our marriage
Must take place before Your Holiness would deign
To countenance and bless our coronation—
Gives me the greater boldness to expect,
That this apparent invalidity
Will, by the Sov'reign Pontiff's own decision,
Be shown to be apparent only, and in
No wise a nullifying or a fatal flaw.
The Emperor has been so wrought upon by
Certain persons whose influence and malice
Are alike so unbounded, that I am filled
With apprehensions for the future. Father,
Be gracious! Maintain the holy dignity
Of that which was in every point ordered
By thy supreme authority itself, and
Is a broken-hearted woman's only hope.
Pronounce my marriage now indissoluble!
To-night, when all my enemies are gathered,
And when the Emperor and I are seated,
And when thy words, so publicly delivered,
Can never in the future be denied, speak!
To-morrow it will be too late. *To-night*, speak! "

  . . . .

 (*Crushes the letter.*)
Malediction!

Fouché.

      Don't swear, Madame.   Do you not
See, that as His Holiness will not declare
Any such thing, and we have got possession
Of this dear quibble of technicality
To work with now, we can afford to let the
Empress swear, saving our own account that much?

Mme. Murat.

But why will not His Holiness speak out?

Fouché.

Why, for the simple reason, don't you see, that he
Has not received this letter—

Mme. Murat.

          You will not dare—

Fouché.

To keep it, or destroy it?   No, Madame, no!
His Holiness will get it.   Yes!—to-morrow.

Mme. Murat.

And then, the irregularity, Monsieur:
You think the absence of the parish priest will
Be enough to void the marriage really?

Fouché.

Madame, it does not take so much in these days
To unlock wedlock!   There, they are coming now.

Enter CAULAINCOURT, *numerous ushers, attendants, and officers in uniform. Arrangements for the approach of the Court.*

(*Exeunt* FOUCHÉ *and* MME. MURAT.

Caulaincourt.

Advise the Emperor that all is ready.

(*Exeunt Officers.*
(*The* EMPEROR's *approach is announced successively by ushers stationed without. The Imperial March is played.*)

A Chamberlain.

(*At the door.*)
The Emperor.

Several Courtiers.

The Emperor!   Make way there !

Enter the immediate members of the Court: TALLEYRAND, FOUCHÉ, MARSHALS MACDONALD *and* NEY, JOSEPH BONAPARTE, YVAN, *Courtiers,* JOSEPHINE *attended by* MMES. MURAT, DE RÉMUSAT, HORTENSE, *etc., etc. Ladies-in-waiting, in stately procession. Last of all,* NAPOLEON, *in the magnificent coronation robes ; he ascends the throne and sits,*[61] *attended by pages in green and lace.*)

Napoleon.

His Holiness proves none too hospitable.
Somebody there, advise him that we are come.

Are not his ill-concealed rebukes in private
Enough, but we must suffer them in public?

Enter Cardinal Fesch.

Fesch.

The Holy Father being much fatigued——[65]

Napoleon.

Keeps
The Court waiting?　Uncle, this is too much!

Josephine.

Pray,
Bonaparte, be patient.　His Holiness has
Earned our everlasting gratitude to-day.[66]

Fesch.

The Holy Father comes immediately.

An Usher.

Way for His Holiness, Pope Pius Seventh!

Enter Pius VII. *clad in simple white cassock*[67] *and
without ceremony or attendants.　All, save* Napoleon, *kneel for his blessing.　He goes to his
throne.*

Napoleon.

Your Holiness was not advised, it seems, of
Our consent to make our first imperial
Visit one which would prove our deep devotion
To His sacred person?

Pius VII.

Nay, we were indeed
Advised of Your Imperial Majesties'
Most laudable intention of piously
Accepting our earnest prayers to honour
Us, before the world, in this first reception.
We more than welcome you, dear royal children,
And lovingly bestow upon you jointly
The Apostolic Benediction.

Josephine.

Amen !

Napoleon.

With which we now proceed to the important
Ceremonies which demand our presence—
   (*Rises.*)

Josephine.

What !

You will not withdraw without the benefit
Of hearing from himself those venerable
Counsels which have been promised to us by the
Holy Father?

Pius VII.

If it be possible, we
Most humbly beg that our dear son bear with us
While, at this august time, we inculcate those
Principles which can alone secure to him
And to his throne a lasting benediction.

Napoleon.

(*Sitting again.*)
So be it then ; but it were scarcely fitting
That we be catechized in public—

Fouché.

(*Aside to* TALLEYRAND.)   Now watch !

Talleyrand.

I pity the old man—I was a bishop.

Pius VII.

And much less fitting was it, certainly, that [68]
In the eyes of all the world, and at a time
Which history will take to the remotest
Ages, we should have suffered open insult
At those hands which we had journied and endured
Unusual hardships, to uplift and bless !

Napoleon.

(*Looking about appealingly.*)
What does he mean ?

Josephine.

(*Quietly to* NAPOLEON.)
                    He means the Coronation.

Napoleon.

Your Holiness has reference to to-day ?

Pius VII.

Aye! To the fact that at the sacred moment
Of his coronation, before God's altar,
In presence of the Holy Gospels, and of
The world, the Emperor proved false, wantonly
Broke his oath, and added sacrilege to his—[69]

Napoleon.

By Heaven! I cannot brook such—

Josephine.

(*Grasping* NAPOLEON'S *arm.*)   For God's sake!

Fesch.

(*To the* POPE.)
Anger him not, Your Holiness.

Talleyrand.

Pray do not!

Mme. Murat.

(*Aside to* FOUCHÉ.)
Do keep them at it—'twill help, Monsieur Fouché.

Napoleon.

Have we not turned the very wheels of custom [70]
Back over centuries, and startled all the
World, by resurrecting from oblivion
This ancient papal privilege of crowning
Kings? What other monarch in five hundred years

Has similarly honoured what other Pope?
The Fisherman, forgotten, ignored, despised,
Mumbling his offices beside the Tiber,
Might never have been heard of in his old *rôle*
Of the dispenser of all earthly crowns, had
Not we ourself, out of our filial love,
Invited him to grace our coronation!
Is it for this most singular and touching
Mark of our devotion, that we are taunted
With a breach of faith?

Pius VII.

It was upon the most
Sincere and solemn protestations of Your
Majesty, that God had put it in your heart
To make this tardy recognition of the
Most ancient privileges and dignities
Of Peter's See, that we, alas! consented,
Not, as you say, to grace a coronation,
But to confer a crown.[51]

Talleyrand.

(*To* Fouché.)   That is delicious!
It makes one feel a thousand years of age.

Napoleon.

Well?

If there were, then, some slight misunderstanding,
As to the trifling point of just who crowned us,
We beg Your Holiness will overlook it.

Monsieur de Talleyrand, you were the master [72]
Of the ceremonies : was it, or was it
Not intended, that we should crown ourself? Come.

Talleyrand.

Sire, it was this way planned. It was decided,
After most careful study of all ancient [73]
Ritualists, that after the blessing of
The crown it must be placed upon your head by
No one but His Holiness himself.

Pius VII.

Else, how——

Napoleon.

Then it was ill-arranged. See that it be not
So arranged again.

Pius VII.

(*To* FESCH.) He mocks us, Cardinal.

Napoleon.

Banish these clouds of mere misunderstanding,
And in the minutes which we happily can
Be the guests and dutiful attendants of
Your Holiness, bestow upon our new-born
Dynasty the blessings of your counsels.

Pius VII.

Well,
Take an old man's blessing, and without further
Words, hasten to give the populace who crowd

The palace courts, the wished-for presence of their
Emperor.   Cardinal, lend us your arm.
   (*Begins to withdraw.*)

Josephine.

(*Starting up.*)
But, will the Holy Father not first grant the
Most devoted of his children's earnest wish ?

Pius VII.

Our daughter would have something at our hands ?

Josephine.

                                                     Yes,
Holy Father, from my soul I beg it now.

Pius VII.

And we shall grant it, daughter—what is it ?

Mme. Murat.

(*To* Fouché.)
Can you not stop this in some way—and quickly ?

Fouché.

Sh-h !   Sh-h !

Josephine.

   Your Holiness has not forgotten ?

Mme. Murat.

(*To* Fouché.)
Don't be a coward !   Stop her before—

Fouché.

Sh-h! Sh-h!

Josephine.

We begged that at this hour Your Holiness would
Graciously consent to ask His Majesty
To wreathe about our diadem the laurel
Of his love, by formally pronouncing his
Complete accord with the decision of Your
Holiness upon a certain vitally
Important point.

 (*The Pope is confused, but tries to recall the point
  and reseats himself.*)

    Wherefore, we shall withdraw in
Order that Your Holiness may with perfect
Freedom elucidate the sacred question.

Napoleon.

We like not all this mystery.

Josephine.

 (*Rising and going toward door.*)
     But trust us!
Come, Mesdames, all of you, attend us. Adieu!
 (*Exeunt all the ladies. MME. MURAT scowls at
  FOUCHÉ as she passes, who signals reassur-
  ance to her.*)

Napoleon.

We have not certainly so grudgingly in
All these years granted our wife's petitions, that
She must needs employ the intercessions of
Another.   But she has chosen well indeed.
We grant it, be it what it may : What is it?

Pius VII.

In truth the ceremonies of this great day
Have so fatigued us, that we cannot recall
Just what it is that our dear daughter wishes.[74]

Napoleon.

Ha! ha! ha! ha! Since we have granted it, we
Have no doubt that our imperial wife
Will readily forgive that.

Pius VII.

                    Her manner seemed
To give the question grave importance in her
Eyes, and it much grieves us that we cannot speak.
We beg that word be instantly brought hither
From our dear child to this intent.

Napoleon.
                    To-morrow.

Pius VII.

She seemed to feel that it must be done now.

Fouché.

Sire.

Napoleon.

Monsieur Fouché.

Fouché.

If it were not considered
Too impertinent, I might suggest that what
Was evidently weighing upon the mind
Of Her Imperial Majesty was her
Solicitude over the promised pardons.[75]

Pius VII.

True! True!   Of course, of course!   We have that surest
Warning of old age—decay of memory.
Your Majesty, this morning we were implored
By our beloved and most Christian daughter,
To beg from your august and charitable
Heart the pardon of all prisoners of state.

Napoleon.

Granted by all means—of course with such reserve
As shall be found to be quite necessary
For our imperial policy.

Many Voices.

Bravo!

Napoleon.

And now to the festivities which wait us!

(*He rises and all proceed to withdraw. Immediately behind* NAPOLEON, *at the end of the procession, walks the* POPE. *Exeunt Omnes,* L.

Enter MME. MURAT *at* R., *cautiously.*

Mme. Murat.

Ha! ha! ha! ha! ha! ha! ha! ha! ha! ha! ha!

(*Exit* L.

CURTAIN.

ACT II.

HIGH-NOON AND AFTER.—1807.

ACT II.

SCENE 1.—*A room in Finkenstein Castle, at night.*[56]

DISCOVERED—RUSTAN *asleep upon the floor in front of a huge wood-fire.*[57] CONSTANT *examining* NAPOLEON'S *unopened mail. Tables, etc., etc.*

(*The Castle bell tolls midnight slowly, and RUS-TAN turns and mutters in his sleep.*)

Constant.

Midnight! Rustan, where did the Emperor go?
    (*Looks over the letters curiously.*)
Rustan, I say—where did the Emperor go?
How that dog sleeps!—The last trump will not wake him,
Unless the Emperor lies in the next grave,
And he suspects that the Archangel's feelings
Are not entirely friendly to his master.
Rustan, I say! There!
    (*Fires his pistol.*)
                He does not turn a hair.
Oh! well!
    (*Looks at letters.*)
           Ah! this one is from Monsieur Fouché.
He must not read it till he has had at least

Three cups of coffee. Monsieur de Talleyrand!
Monsieur de Talleyrand would best wait also.
Monsieur de Talleyrand has fall'n into the
Habit lately of writing something so near
The truth, that neither the Emperor nor I
Enjoy it. Best sleep on you, my Talleyrand!
Ah! One from Josephine! Two! Three! Jeal-
ousy.
Would one hear from his wife, let it be rumoured
That—but never mind! This one I can't make out.
It smells! ah sweet! Josephine must have smelled
it.
If he is cross and hungry, he shall read that
First. This one is from Monsieur——

Rustan.

(*Starting up.*)   Who's there? Who's there?

Constant.

Nobody, Rustan?

Rustan.

There is. I heard a step.

Constant.

Did you, indeed? Did you not hear a pistol,
And talking, and——

Rustan.

Rustan hears only danger:
Rustan is sure he heard a woman's footstep!
(*Creeps to the door to listen.*)

Constant.

Rustan has a discriminating ear, then!
Danger, indeed! Ha! ha! A woman's footstep!

Rustan.

She is upon the stairs; she has reached the top;
She comes this way! Rustan is very cunning.
Rustan knows how. Rustan will cut her tongue out.

Constant.

And so, of course, avoid all of the danger.
   (*A knock is heard.*)
Back to your kennel, dog! I will receive her.
Who knocks? (*Silence.*)
   Who knocks? Rustan, be quiet! Who knocks?

Mme. Walewska.

(*From without.*)
One whom the Emperor's command has brought
   here.[73]

Rustan.

Rustan knows danger: he knew it was a she.

Constant.

The hour is late. Madame will pardon caution?
Would Madame write her name upon this paper?
   (*Slips a sheet of paper under the door.*) (*Aside.*)
Now we shall see who wrote this scented letter.
   (*Takes up the scented note from the table. The
      sheet of paper is pushed back under the door.
      Reads.*)

"Marie, Countess Walewska, obediently."
    (*Aside.*)
Ah! ha! The same! I knew that something fe-
    male
Was in his mind when I began to dress him.
Madame!
    (*Aloud.*)

Mme. Walewska.
    Yes! Open instantly!

Constant.
                 Is madame
Looked for by His Imperial Majesty?

Mme. Walewska.
He sent three members of his staff to fetch me.

Constant.
Will Madame enter? Madame's most humble slave!

Enter Mme. Walewska, *muffled, veiled, and covered
with snow.*

Will Madame permit me to assist her? No?

Mme. Walewska.
The Emperor's private room: which way? He
    wished
Me to proceed to it immediately.

Constant.

This way, if Madame pleases. Rustan, make way!
(*Exit* MME. WALEWSKA *into* NAPOLEON's *room.*
Our little friend from Warsaw, I dare wager!
No wonder that he drank twelve cups of coffee,
Ruined three razors and made me cut him twice;[79]
Called Marshal Soult a —— something not very nice,
And kept his *aides-de-camp* about half crazy
Commanding and then countermanding blunders![80]
These women! Oh! these women! Now, as for
  me—
(*Having returned, and looking at the letters.*)
What? One for me? Eh! From Paris? From
  Babette!
(*Tears it open, and dances about with joy.*)
How's this? She's coming here, and she is on her
  way!
Great heavens! She may arrive at any hour!
If she should come at night! This night! Oh!
  women!

Rustan.

(*Starting up from sleep.*)
Rustan hears danger.

Constant.

      Not again? Horrible!
(*Rustan listens and then falls asleep again.*)
Thank heaven! He was mistaken! Oh, these
  women!
(*Sits and continues to look over the letters.*)

More from the Empress? Who has been telling her?
No one, perhaps, for jealousy has instincts.
At any rate, I never have to advise
Madame Constant: she *knows!* Oh! doesn't she?
    Hark!
    (NAPOLEON's *voice heard without.*)

Enter NAPOLEON *rapidly, covered with snow.* RUSTAN
    does not awake.

Napoleon.

Coffee, Constant! Rustan, inquire who is the
Aide-de-camp! Constant, what are you leaving
    for? [81]
    (CONSTANT *returns.*)   (*Exit* RUSTAN.

Constant.

For coffee, Sire.

Napoleon.

    Do you intend to leave me
Standing, soaked through? You blockhead! Where
    is Rustan?
    (NAPOLEON *moves about while* CONSTANT *tries to*
    remove his coat.)

Constant.

Rustan has gone to inquire what *aide-de-camp*—

Napoleon.

What *are* you trying to do to me, Constant?

Constant.

(*Aside.*)

I never saw him quite so bad.   Oh, women!

(NAPOLEON *sits by the table and begins to look over
      the papers, etc.   Stretches out his hand at
      side several times.*)

Napoleon.

Why, in the fiend's name, don't you give it to me?

Constant.

Give you what, Sire!

Napoleon.

My coffee!   What time is it?

Constant.

Past midnight, Sire.

Napoleon.

So late?   Then go and see if
The Division Officers have not come in.

Constant.

The coffee, Sire?

Napoleon.

Yes, give it to me, Constant!

Constant.

Shall I go fetch it first?

Napoleon.

Have you not fetched it?
Go, blockhead! The simpleton must be in love.
(*Exit* Constant. Napoleon *looks at letters.*)

Re-enter Constant *with the coffee.*

Well, well, who is the *aide-de-camp* on duty?

Constant.

(*Arranges coffee near the fire.* Napoleon *sits to
drink.*)
I went for coffee, Sire : it was Rustan that —

Napoleon.

True, true, my good Constant.

Constant.

(*Aside.*)   The smell of coffee
Is my best friend. Just hear him : "My *good* Con-
stant!"
(Napoleon *muses and sips coffee.*)

Napoleon.

Constant!

Constant.

Here, Sire.

Napoleon.

The courier brought letters?

Constant.

All these, Sire. Shall I read? Four from the
    Empress.

Napoleon.

Four! say you? Oh! yes, I was expecting—four!

Constant.

(*Aside.*)
That's true! Or forty, for that matter ——

Napoleon.

And? And?

Constant.

And one from — from, from — Warsaw, I should
    think, Sire.

Napoleon.

Eh! Warsaw? Why do you say from Warsaw, eh?

Constant.

(*Carries letter to him.*)
By—by—the perfume of it, Sire. I never
Smelt anything like it—except in Warsaw.
    (NAPOLEON *reads the note.*)

Napoleon.

(*After musing a moment.*)
Constant, a lady may arrive at any time.
An elderly dependent on our charity,

Whom we have offered to protect and harbour
For a while. There! did you hear a step, Constant?   .

Constant.

No, Sire! (*Aside.*) Heavens! the elderly dependent
Must be kept quiet, till I can get her out.
    (*Returning from the door where he listened.*)
I hear no footstep, Sire. Was she expected?

Napoleon.

At any moment. She must not be allowed
To be seen here. When she arrives conduct her
To the apartment hung with cream-white damask
Near our own room. Under no circumstances
Must she go in my room. You understand me?

Constant.

Perfectly, Sire. (*Sighs.*)
    (*Aside.*)   Why did I not let Rustan
Kill her at sight?—The dog suspected danger.

Napoleon.

Constant, if I mistake not, you always knew—
Yes, fill it, fill it—two lumps—you always knew
All of the serving maids about the palace?

Constant.

Sire, not all, not all. I am a married man.

Napoleon.

You told me that Madame Constant was jealous.

Constant.

She was, Sire—madly jealous ; but without cause.

Napoleon.

Of course, of course ; since you declare that you knew
Only—how many did you say ? and not all
Of the pretty girls, it was illogical
In Madame to be jealous.   Well, now, Constant,
Among the few whom you did know, remember
You one better than the rest, one more discreet,
One who could be brought here, and who would see,
    hear,
Serve, and do as she was bid, and hold her tongue ?

Constant.

Sire, I do remember just such a creature.

Napoleon.

Her name ?

Constant.

Babette Lacouvier, dark eyes, red——

Napoleon.

Never mind, Constant.   Write the sonnet later.
Babette would come here ? Babette would hold her
    tongue ?

Constant.

Sire, Babette would come.

Napoleon.

And mind her own affairs ?

Constant.

Sire, I have known Babette to remain quiet
For half an hour.   (*Aside.*)   Asleep !

Napoleon.

Send for her at once !
Another cup.   What other letters are there ?

Constant.

One from Monsieur de Talleyrand.

Napoleon.

To-morrow !

Constant.

From Monsieur Fouché.

Napoleon.

Day after to-morrow !

Constant.

Four from Her Majesty, the Empress.

Napoleon.

(*Aside.*)   Never !

Enter RUSTAN, *who lies down at door.*

Rustan !   Rustan !   Awake the villain, Constant.

Constant.

But how, Sire ?

Napoleon.

By siege, by—

Rustan.

(*Starting up.*)   Rustan hears danger !

Constant.

(*Aside.*)
Again ? Confound that elderly dependent !
(*Coughs and stamps about.*)

Napoleon.

Rustan, found you the *aide-de-camp* on duty ?

Rustan.

Sire, Rustan obeys. Rustan found *aide-de-camp*—
On duty ? What is that ? No understand, Sire.
The Monsieur *aide-de-camp* was playing—

Napoleon.

                              Duty !
A game, Rustan, which we have taught our soldiers
So well, that they out-play all others at it !
Constant, advise the *aide-de-camp* that he will
Go at once to the headquarters of the Prince
Neufchatel, five leagues away, and be back here
Not later than sunrise to-morrow morning.
He will deliver these despatches to the
Prince in person.
      (*Gives packet.*)   (*Exit* Constant.
            And it's a devilish night.
Our new game, Duty, is not an easy one ;

They win who stake glory and France upon it!

(RUSTAN *falls asleep.* NAPOLEON *sits before the fire.*)

Four letters from my wife! What have I done *now?*
Junot informs me that Josephine finds ways[81]
Of getting consolation in my absence.
The jealousy of women does not depend,
It seems, so much upon their virtue as their
Pride. She can become the scandal of the town,
And yet write lectures on inconsistency!
Poor Josephine! Not so poor either; not when
One remembers the natural history
Of jealousy as it is writ in ruin.

(*Rises and walks about.*)

The fall of no man is a true fall at all!
It is a ruin rather: the long result
Of battling against odds, and, single hearted,
Encountering the onslaught of chill distrust.
No man begins but as a virtuous child.
Nor dreams of sin until he is charged with it!
Man is a man, and by deliberate choice
Never is less. But into his good heart
This cursèd world flings the pestiferous seeds
Of unbelief: not unbelief in God, for
Hell might proclaim itself, and so an end;
But unbelief in man! At Castiglione
I said to a Lieutenant of Dragoons: "There!
Caulaincourt, I wish that battery taken!
Take it with twenty men!" "General," he said,
"Two hundred could not!" "But twenty can," I
                     said.

He took the battery.   Before St. Jean d'Acre
There was a dangerous sally-port to close.
A stripling near my side begged for permission.
A score cried "No!"   "Boy, can you do it, think
   you?"
"General, I can, if you believe in me!"
"I do!"   The boy was mangled into pieces,
But the port was closed.   And it is always thus.
We desperately grasp at good opinion,
Which is the Creed men have concerning others,
And as a rule we do no better and no
Worse than others say we will.   Oh! Josephine!
Oh! jealousy! Oh! women, do ye not know
That man, being made of confidence and trust,
Rises or falls as these art meted to him?
The bride who sets a watch upon her husband,
Has branded him and set a premium on
Infidelity.   Well, what says Josephine?
   (*Opens one of the letters.*)

Rustan.

Rustan hears danger!   Rustan hears woman's step.
   (*A knock is heard.*)

Napoleon.

It must be Marie!   Open the door, Rustan!

Enter BABETTE, *muffled and agitated.*

Babette.

   (*Throwing off her hood, etc.*)
Sire!   I thought—I was told really—

Napoleon.

Babette!
How in the name of all the saints came you here?

Babette.

Sire, it was in this way, Sire.   Monsieur Constant
Wrote me that Your Imperial Majesty
Had come to Finkenstein and would need servants.
Monsieur Constant has probably advised Your
Majesty that I was cruelly discharged
From the Imperial service—has he—Sire?

Napoleon.

No!   Monsieur Constant never conveys bad news.

Babette.

(*Courtesies profoundly.*)
Yes, Sire, discharged!   And all the spiteful doing
Of Madame Constant.   So then Monsieur Constant
Wrote me to come at once to Finkenstein, so—

Napoleon.

So that Madame Constant might feel relieved, eh?

Babette.

Oh, no!   Sire, no!   So that I might find service.
And Monsieur Constant—

Napoleon.

Oh!   I see now, Babette:
So that you might find service and Monsieur—

Babette.

Sire !

Napoleon.

Pack off to bed, child.   To-morrow we will see.
Avoid the corridors : no place for women.
That is our own room.   Pass through it to the left,
And you will find a little private entrance
Into a fine apartment.   Sleep there to-night.
   (BABETTE *courtesies and backs into the room.   Exit.*
Rustan ! Rustan ! That dog hears nothing harmless.

Rustan.

(*Raising himself on his elbow.*)
Rustan hears danger.   Rustan hears women's words.

Napoleon.

Save us from them and make an end of evil.

Enter CONSTANT.   RUSTAN *asleep again.*

Napoleon.

Constant !

Constant.

Here, Sire !

Napoleon.

Constant, who is in my room ?

Constant.

(*Aside.*)
That black dog has been telling—
   (*Aloud.*)   Nobody, Sire.

Napoleon.

You lie, you rascal! Come, now, who is in there?

Constant.

A lady, sire!

Napoleon.

Would you not say she was one?

Constant.

By all means, Sire. Heaven forbid that I should—

Napoleon.

Why did you not confess to me, you scoundrel?

Constant.

Confess what, Sire?

Napoleon.

About Babette, you booby.
So you did send for her?

Constant.

I will send now, Sire.

Napoleon.

Pray do not, Constant.

Constant.

I will to-morrow, Sire.

Napoleon.

Do, and, Monsieur, suppose that you now tell us

Why you admitted Madame in our absence?
She had to take the cream-white damask *boudoir*.
Now, if the elderly dependent, of whom
We spoke, should happen to arrive, pray, Monsieur,
What should we do? Eh?

Constant.

It would be awkward, Sire.
(*Aside.*)
Heavens! There is some elderly dependent, then!
Sire, I ventured to admit her on the ground
That it would please your Majesty.

Napoleon.

A lover
Speaks there, so I forgive you.

Rustan.

(*Starting up.*)   Rustan hears danger!

Napoleon.

(*Aside.*)
It is Marie, at last!

Constant.

(*Aside.*)
Babette! It must be!
(*A knock is heard at door from* NAPOLEON's *room.*)

Napoleon.

You see, Constant, that she received your letter.

Constant.

My letter!　Your Majesty has been deceived!
Rustan has told your Majesty a falsehood!
Babette is not in there.

Napoleon.

　　　　Fie!　Fie!　Lothario!
Come!　You are not talking to Madame Constant,
So you might tell the truth without this blushing!

Constant.

Sire, she was muffled; Rustan mistook the form.
Sire, it was not Babette : it was another!

Napoleon.

You shall see, Constant!

Constant.

　　　　Your Majesty will see!

Napoleon.

Come in!　Open the door there!

Enter Countess Walewska *and* Babette *in light gowns.*

　　　　　　Marie!
Constant.
　　　　　　　　Babette!
　(Babette *courtesies to the* Emperor.)

Babette.

Sire, may I be lady's maid to fair Madame?

Constant.

(*Hurriedly pushing* BABETTE *to door.*)

Sh! Sh! Babette! get out of here!

Babette.

(*At the door.*) Sire, may I?

(*Exeunt* CONSTANT *and* BABETTE.

Napoleon.

My darkest hours are welcome, for it is then
Invariably that you appear, Marie.
Come to me, girl. You must be cold and weary.
So! Be warmed, be rested here, upon my heart.
My letter reached you—

Mme. Walewska.

Yesterday, Sire, at noon.

Napoleon.

And you are here so soon?—

Mme. Walewska.

It seemed long ages,
And I may stop here, Sire, a long, long—[86]

Napoleon.

Always!

Mme. Walewska.

Sire!

Napoleon.

You have convinced me, child, that happiness
Consists in being absolutely trusted.
Look up at me! Marie, in these two blue eyes

I found the key to the profound enigma
Of myself.   Life of my soul!   Look up at me!
Count up the elementals of which your heart
Is made.   Love free from jealousy.   Confidence
Calling for no more proof than is consistent
With its own sweet self.   The giving of oneself
For no return, no calculated *quid pro*
Quo ; but for the sheer delight of worshipping :
Wide, holy, generosity of judgment,
Which is blind purposely, appealing ever
From Philip in his cups, to Philip sober.
A deep, pure, tranquil, and unmerited love !
Wrap that about the chaos of a broken
Heart, and it becomes transfigured into peace.
To thoughts of such love a man will stretch his arms
Out from the darkness, the passion, and the pain.
Marie, the night is dark and cold : Sing to me !

Mme. Walewska.
(*Fetches her lute : sits at his feet.*)
What shall I sing, Sire?

Napoleon.
Sing what you sang that night.

Mme. Walewska.
(*Sings.*)

I.

Out of the North ! [87]
Out from the cold and the bleak desolation ;
Out from the deathly chill haunts of despair ;

Out from the echoes of dead consolation ;
Out of the North !
From the terrible sea :
From the hungry wolf's yelp ;
For a chance to be free,
For the sunlight and help !
Flee from the North !

II.

Into the South !
Into the garden-nooks warm joys concealing ;
Into the scent-laden bowers of Love ;
Into the exquisite rapture of feeling ;
Into the South !
For the hum of the bee ;
For the long afternoon ;
For what lovers can see
By the light of the moon !
Flee to the South !

(*Here* NAPOLEON *rises and walks about. At the table he picks up* JOSEPHINE's *letters, and returns to the fireplace holding them in his hands.*)

Napoleon.

Don't stop, Marie, please.

Mme. Walewska.

What letters are those, Sire ?

Napoleon.

Unhappy ones—but sing!

Mme. Walewska.

You have not read them, Sire?

Napoleon.

Not yet, not yet. Forget them, Sweet, and sing, sing.

Mme. Walewska.

(*Sings*).

III.

Out from yourself!
Out from the past with its wrecks and contrition;
Out from the dull discontentment of now;
Out from the future's false-speaking ambition;
Out from yourself.
For your broken-heart's rest;
For the peace which you crave;
For the end of your quest;
For the love which can save!
Come! Come to me!

(NAPOLEON *throws the letters into the fire unread.*)[88]

Napoleon.

(*Muses long.*)
Marie!—Out from *myself?*

Mme. Walewska.

Sire, to me! to me!

Napoleon.

(*Taking her in his arms.*)
Do not sing any more to-night.   Let us be
Quiet now and watch the fire burn out.

Mme. Walewska.

Yes, Sire!

(*They stand and watch.*)

Curtain.

Scene 2.—*A terrace of Fontainebleau.   Afternoon.*[89]

Discovered—Hortense *and* Madame de Rémusat *sitting upon a garden seat.   Back of the stone balustrade of the terrace groups of Courtiers and Ladies pass and repass.*

Hortense.

Alas!   Madame de Rémusat, I cannot.
You say that he is at the zenith of his
Power.   He has come back to France a hero,
And one might almost say, he is almighty.
They will fawn upon him; kiss his very feet;
Fouché and Talleyrand will vie with Murat
In offering incense.   Bah!   I know them all!
No, no, Madame de Rémusat, I cannot
Blind my eyes to what is passing.   Napoleon
Is a miserable man.

Mme. de Rémusat.
> You mean unhappy?

Hortense.
I do, Madame de Rémusat. And for the
Reason, that he no longer loves my mother.

Mme. de Rémusat.
An enemy has done this. All will soon be
Explained, and love will then return upon the
Wings of confidence.[90]

Hortense.
> Madame de Rémusat,
Love often dies after the marriage service;[91]
But did you ever hear that any woman
Was loved a second time by the same lover?

Mme. de Rémusat.
Forgive me, dear Hortense, your Majesty sees
Everything through the discolouring glass
Of your own sorrow. You have confided in
Me as your friend. Your life is wretched. Your
    child [92]
Is dead. Your husband—— [93]

Hortense.
> Spare me, for God's sake, Claire!

Mme. de Rémusat.
Yes! yes! forgive me! But will you not at least
Try to persuade the Emperor to listen?

Hortense.

I talked with him about two hours this morning.
The same old story !   He reverences me [94]
Above all women, and even as a child,
Would listen to my arguments with patience.
My influence became so great, you know, that
Gossip soon was whispering—you know, you know ! [95]
Well, for two hours he listened with all patience ;
But, Claire, dear, no logic ever yet forced love.

Mme. de Rémusat.

Madame Murat has been insinuating,
That at the bottom of the difficulty
There is a——

Hortense.

          Woman ?   No very deep guess, that !
There is a woman in the case—certainly !

Mme. de Rémusat.

There have been others of whom he has grown tired, [96]
And come back from, to the forgiving Empress !

Hortense.

Yes, for they were passing fancies ; but this one
Is the only woman whom he ever loved. [97]

Mme. de Rémusat.

He will not bring her here ?

Hortense.

          She is here now, Claire ! [98]

Enter NAPOLEON, *rapidly.*

Napoleon.

Oh! here you are! I have been looking for you.
What, in the devil's name, Hortense, has happened?
I have filled Fontainebleau with half of Paris:
I have invited all my friends and neighbours;
I have provided music, entertainment,
Games; I have laid by the starch and dignity
Of Emperor, in hope of being simply host.
And now, what happens? You hang about in groups,
You whisper, you act as if you all were at
My funeral. This is the celebration
Of my victories, and not my funeral! [30]

Hortense.

(*Seeing* JOSEPHINE *about to pass outside the ter-
.race.*)
Sire, upon the face of her who is about
To pass, you might discover the true reason.
(JOSEPHINE *passes slowly, musing.*)

Napoleon.

Josephine! I felt as much! Hortense, wake up.
(*Runs out of the terrace: joins* JOSEPHINE.)
(*Exeunt* NAPOLEON *and* JOSEPHINE.

Hortense.

We really must do something to wake things up.
(*Exeunt* HORTENSE *and* MME. DE RÉMUSAT.

Enter Fouché *and* Mme. Murat. *They cross.*

Fouché.

You say that you are certain that he has brought
Our pretty Polish sweetheart to Fontainebleau?

Mme. Murat.

Most certainly, I do. And now the question [100]
Is, how to arrange to have the dear thing and
The Empress brought face to face. Won't Josephine
Enjoy it?

Fouché.

Immensely! but, how in the world
Can it be brought about? Louis the Fourteenth
Was one thing—Napoleon is another. [101]

Mme. Murat.

True!—
But from all accounts, this new divinity
Does not propose to be shut up in *boudoirs*
All her life.

Fouché.

So much the better. Well, Madame,
Find out this beauty, then, and use her, use her!
(*Exeunt* Fouché *and* Mme. Murat.

Enter Joseph Bonaparte *and numerous Ladies and Gentlemen, who cross, chatting and laughing.*

Joseph.

The Emperor most graciously invites you

All to join him in the theatre at once.
The music has arrived and the performance
Will be begun the moment that the guests have——
(Exeunt omnes.

Enter NAPOLEON, *driving another group of courtiers
ahead of him and followed by* TALLEYRAND.

Napoleon.

Pass on! Pass on! No more of this dejection!
The theatre waits you, friends. The play begins.
Monsieur de Talleyrand, a word with you, please.
(Exeunt omnes except NAPOLEON and TALLEYRAND.

Talleyrand.

Sire, there is no master of ceremonies
Like yourself.
Napoleon.

Perhaps! Ordering fools about
Came naturally to me. Now, Talleyrand,
Prove yourself capable of ruling one fool.

Talleyrand.
Who, Sire?

Napoleon.

Yourself! You have been talking to the Empress?

Talleyrand.

Upon my honour, Sire, I have. What of it?

Napoleon.

This, that she dreams of nothing but of divorce!

Talleyrand.

Divorce, Sire?

Napoleon.

Divorce! Talks of it in her sleep.
Now, Talleyrand, have you turned priest again, that
You must carry tales of our iniquities
To the already quite too jealous Empress?
Eh? Hypocrite? Say, do you go straight from the
Embraces of your own kept mistresses to [102]
Prate of our shortcomings to our poor Empress?

Talleyrand.

Sire! You paralyze me with amazement, Sire!

Napoleon.

If it be possible for you to tell the
Truth, tell it this once in expiation of
Your lifelong lying.[103] The Empress has been told
That we have brought a certain noble lady
To Fontainebleau, and it has so inflamed her
Jealousy, that at this very summit of
Our glory she is about to seek divorce!

Talleyrand.

Ah!—ha!
(*Long pondering.*)

Napoleon.

Well? What do you see in it so deep?

Talleyrand.

Sire, two things! I see Monsieur Fouché, I see
Madame Murat.

Napoleon.

They have been telling, have they?

Talleyrand.

Sire, the Empress seeks no divorce. Alas! she
Fears one. I see the meaning of all this now!

Napoleon.

Then, have the goodness to unfold it to us.

Talleyrand.

Sire, Monsieur Fouché is stirring up the old
Design of the Imperial divorce, for—

Napoleon.

—For some unfathomable purpose, doubtless.

Talleyrand.

—Suggested to him by Her Imperial
Highness, Madame Murat. [104] At all events, this
Is quite clear—what now disturbs the Empress——

Napoleon.

                                                    Is
Not our passion for the noble Countess, eh?
But these maliciously suggested rumours
Of a divorce? This comforts me. Talleyrand,
Find out the Countess now, and personally

Become responsible that she does not for
Any reason appear to-day. And meanwhile
Send the Empress to us.

Talleyrand.
She will come gladly.
(*Exit.*

Enter Caulaincourt, Hortense, Mme. de Rémusat,
Ladies, Joseph Bonaparte, Macdonald, Ney, *Officers, etc., etc.*

Napoleon.

So at last you have decided to enjoy
Yourselves? To prove it, you shall dance before us.
Hortense, we trust your Majesty will honour
Us? Caulaincourt, bid the musicians yonder
Play the new quadrille brought recently from Spain.
That Andalusian music is as sweet
To me as my wife's voice—and what is sweeter? [105]
(*The music begins: they dance.*)

Napoleon.

(*During a pause.*)
Macdonald, take our place. You've done so often.

Macdonald.

Never before, Sire, one-half so willingly.
Your Majesty accepts the substitute?

Hortense.
With
Genuine pleasure, may it please your Grace, but

I expect that her Imperial Majesty,
My mother, is coming with Monsieur Fouché,
And I must be excused when she has reached us,
As she desires my service.   Until then—yours!

> (*They dance.* NAPOLEON *watches. During the
> dancing* FOUCHÉ *and* JOSEPHINE *cross and re-
> cross beyond the balustrade, talking ear-
> nestly.*)

Napoleon.

We thank you, friends, for showing us that France
   is
Not insensible to glory.   Believe us,
Since our return to Paris, after a year
Of war uninterruptedly successful,
And whereby France was made the arbitress of all
The world, we have not heard or seen the slightest
Token of true joy—till now.   We thank you all!

Josephine.

(*From beyond the parapet.*)
A wager has been laid, Sire, on your answers.
Answer me now instinctively, and without
Study.   What woman love you most, Sire?

Napoleon.

                       My wife! [106]

Fouché.

In explanation, Sire, I——

Josephine.

Don't interrupt!
What woman, Sire, do you esteem the highest?

Napoleon.

The best house-keeper.　Because——

Josephine.

Never mind why.
And whom do you place first among all women?

Napoleon.

She who bears children to her——
　　　(JOSEPHINE *screams and exit.*)
　　　　　　　　　　Monsieur Fouché,
Is this a time for harping upon that string?
Cannot we snatch one hour of quiet pleasure,
But you, yes, all of you, harass, torment us?
Go, Caulaincourt, and find the Empress for us.
The rest enjoy yourselves—not in our presence!
　　　(*Exeunt Omnes, except* NAPOLEON.)

　　　·　　　·　　　·　　　·　　　·　　　·

Call no man happy till he is in his grave![107]
I wanted Europe : Europe is at my feet!
And what is at my feet?　A mole-hill—Europe![108]
I wanted men to fear me, bow to my will.
Bah! they would cringe about me anyhow!　For[109]
Only good kings are not served.　A good king
　　is a[110]

King who is ruined.   But against me Destiny
Suffers no opposition to avail.   And
Yet what am I?   A superstitious coward,
Who dares not put away a wife he loves not!
And who cannot forget the exiled Bourbons; [111]
Who cannot break God's laws with a light con-
   science!
I, free?   I, great?   Not while Josephine and God
And Louis the Eighteenth have power to haunt me!
Not every man can be an atheist [112]
Who would be.   Else, what could thwart my Poli-
   cy? [113]

Enter JOSEPHINE, *agitated.*

Josephine.

Sire!

Napoleon.

You never called me Sire until to-day. [114]
I do not like it, Josephine, from your lips.
   (*Kisses her.*)

Josephine.

My husband!   Bonaparte!

Napoleon.

Something has happened?

Josephine.

Oh! much, much, much!   Monsieur Fouché has
   told me

Everything.   At last my awful doom is here!
I have been yours eleven years, Napoleon,
And now I am to be divorced?

Napoleon.
Who said so?

Josephine.
Spare yourself, Bonaparte.   Who could have said so
Without your knowledge and consent?   Who would
    have
Dared?   Monsieur Fouché said so!   All France says
    so!
Have I not eyes, or ears, or a breaking heart?
Must I be told what all the world sees plainly?[115]
You want a child: I cannot bear one for you,
And so—and so—and ——
    (*Breaks down.*)

Napoleon.
Whoever told you that
Lied in his throat, and I will cut his tongue out.

Josephine.
Oh! Bonaparte, for God's sake, don't divorce me!
If it must be so, love whom you will, but don't
Divorce me!   I have put up with much, and now
I shall endure whatever added insults
You may choose; but spare me this.   All but Divorce!

Napoleon.
I swear it, Josephine.   Come to me, darling.

Now tell me what Monsieur Fouché has dared to
Say.　He shall pay well for it, the miscreant![116]

Josephine.

Sire, I thank you from the bottom of my heart.
The Minister of General Police, then,
Began by asking, if I had been informed,
That you had brought a beautiful young mistress
Here to Fontainebleau.

Napoleon.

　　　　That Fouché came from hell!
I hope you told him that he lied, Josephine?

Josephine.

I did, indeed.　For even a husband is
Not all brute.　No, Bonaparte, I told Monsieur
Fouché that you would not parade your vices
Before my very face, however much you
Might indulge in them behind my back—alas!

Napoleon.

Brava! my wife!　Oh! if you had always shown
Such confidence as that!

Josephine.

　　　　But Monsieur Fouché
Laughed at my incredulity; gave me the
Woman's name—Countess Walewska—and also
Said that she was here at Fontainebleau.　*Is she?*

Napoleon.

There never was a liar equal to that
Monsieur Fouché—yes, Monsieur de Talleyrand!
And it is to these two inimitable
Liars that I am forced to show the very
Beatings of my heart? Bah! I will show them now!

Josephine.

But what Monsieur Fouché told me about this
Paramour, was not the deepest cause of my
Distress, Napoleon. Marriage is not a bar
In these loose days to love—if it ever was,
Since love, true love is free and brooks no "shalt
    nots;"
But what he told me, about my barrenness,
That, broke my heart. Because I knew, Napoleon,
That in addition to that sublime instinct
Which makes a man desire to be a father,
You have the added yearnings of ambition
To have a son to whom to leave the Empire!

Napoleon.

You put your finger upon the naked nerve
Which causes all the anguish of my soul. Don't!

Josephine.

Alas! My husband, my pity for myself
Is lost in that I feel for you.

Napoleon.

Josephine !

Josephine.

It was to prove to me that your desire for
Children was paramount, and must before long
Lead to my divorce, that he proposed to me
That cruel jest of asking, whom you thought first.
And when you answered, that you esteemed her first
Who could bear children, did you not see the leer,
The mocking leer of triumph, upon his face?
Nor hear that cursed laugh of his which laughs not ?[117]

Napoleon.

He has out-devilled his own deviltry, and
He shall pay for it, now! Ho! there, somebody!

Enter a PAGE.

Paper and pens, without delay.   (*Exit* PAGE.
                              Josephine !

Josephine.

Sire !

Napoleon.

Hortense, your daughter, taught me to believe ;[118]
But you have taught me something much more noble.
You have taught all of us how great souls suffer!

Re-enter the PAGE.

And you shall see now how profound my thanks are.
   (*Sits on the bench and writes. Then reads aloud.*)
                         (*Exit the* PAGE.

Now listen, Josephine.
                   " Monsieur Fouché : In
The last fortnight I have heard too much about
Your foolish actions. And it is time for you
To put an end to them, and to stop meddling,
Directly or indirectly, in matters
Which in no way concern you. It is my wish."[119]

.   .   .   .   .   .

There ! Do you think that that will finish Fouché ?

Josephine.

If you could know my gratitude, Napoleon,
And the relief which your assurances have
Brought me, you would feel repaid. Kiss me, my
   King.

Napoleon.

And now you rest here, while I deliver this
In person. Madame de Rémusat will come
To attend you. Adieu, sweetheart !   (*Exit.*

Josephine.

(*Drops upon the bench.*)
                    He loves me !

Enter MME. MURAT *and* COUNTESS WALEWSKA.

Mme. Murat.

Ah!   Her Imperial Majesty alone.
Allow me to present the Emperor's dear
Friend, who is to live with us at Fontainebleau.
Your Majesty, this is Countess Walewska !
　　　(JOSEPHINE *tries to rise, but falls back fainting.*)

CURTAIN.

ACT III.

THE EVENING SACRIFICE.—1809.

ACT III.

SCENE 1.—*A Secret Boudoir at Saint-Cloud. Night.*

DISCOVERED—JOSEPHINE *and* TALLEYRAND *cautiously looking in at the door. Before another door leading to inner room,* RUSTAN *lies asleep upon the floor.*[120]

Talleyrand.

Would it be safe, Your Majesty, to rouse him?

Josephine.

No! He is capable of killing us both;[121]
But he will not disturb us—he knows my step.
If you are sure that this is her room, enter!
 (TALLEYRAND *goes toward door.*)
But hold, Monsieur de Talleyrand! The gossips
Of the Court may have misled you: in which case
Nothing could possibly avert my ruin,
If a suspicion of this espionage
Should reach the Emperor.
 (*Grasping* TALLEYRAND'S *hands.*)
      Are you a true man?

Talleyrand.

The history of my relations with your
Majesty—recall it! Am I a true man?

Is not my presence at this moment in this
Perilous place sufficient answer?   Were I
Not altogether true to the unhappy
Cause which weighs so heavily upon your
Majesty, would I risk everything as
I do now, by playing the spy upon the
Gallantries of my imperial master? [132]

Josephine.

True, Talleyrand!   Of course, of course.   Forgive
  me !

Talleyrand.

Most gracious mistress!   Now we must to the point.
  (*Aside.*)
The devil only knows just how to reach it.
  (*Aloud.*)
Constant assured me that one Babette —

Josephine.

Babette ?

Talleyrand.

I think that was her name——

Josephine.

Never mind.   Go on.

Talleyrand.

Constant assured me that this Babette—Susette—

Josephine.

Babette—I know her !—if I could once get my
Two hands—but never mind !   Proceed !

Talleyrand.

He said that—
Come to think of it, it was Susette, yes—that
Susette—I mean Babette—no, no, Susette—that
She would be here at this hour.   I was a fool
To count upon a woman.

Josephine.

That woman, yes!

Talleyrand.

She was the only one connected with the case.
But, then, it always is the only woman
Whom one has got to trust, that can't be trusted!

Josephine.

And if that vixen had been here, pray tell me,
Just how would she have been of service to us?

Talleyrand.

Why, as a woman!

Josephine.

Monsieur de Talleyrand
Remembers that he was a bishop sometimes :
He mystifies, to prove that he is learnèd.
What are the uses of a woman—Bishop?

Talleyrand.

Three !——

Josephine.

So many? I fancied that when we had
Amused our lords we had fulfilled our function!

Talleyrand.

By no means! Woman is to be made use of
In three ways: first, as a medium for the
Dissemination of important secrets;
Second, as the unfailing vehicle for
Getting what is most confidential published;
And third, as the discriminating agent
Who confides all that she knows to all the world.

Josephine.

And this Babette is recommended to you —

Talleyrand.

As one in whom implicit confidence is
Placed, and therefore one from whom we may
    expect
To learn all that has been confided to her.

Josephine.

Enough, Monsieur! Now to the point! My heart
    breaks.

Talleyrand.

Myriad repentances.

Josephine.

The point! the point!

Monsieur de Talleyrand has piloted me
Here. He tells me that this is the *boudoir* of
My husband's favourite, mysteriously
Hints that this wanton woman can in some way
Save me, a lawful and obedient wife,
From the unutterable shame of a divorce.
And I believed him! Truly despair does make
A woman trustful. If you have any heart,
Come to the point, the point! I cannot longer
Breathe the air of this accursèd place. Good God!

Talleyrand.

Now that Your Majesty is seated, I can
In one word—yes, one word, or at most, two words—

Josephine.

Two words!—then speak them, Monsieur de Talleyrand.

Talleyrand.

The child!

Josephine.

What child?

Talleyrand.

The missing child, of course.

Josephine.

Whose?

Talleyrand.

Your Majesty's!

Josephine.

You mock?

Talleyrand.

On the contrary,
I would forever stop the mouths of those whose
Mocking has now acquired such fatal meaning.
Your Majesty—sweet mistress—open your heart
To me, your oldest servant, your truest friend.
What would forever put an end to all this
Plausible outrage of a divorce?

Josephine.

A child.

Talleyrand.

Your Majesty, the Emperor will shortly
Have a child.[123]

Josephine.

Monster! fiend! Wretch without a heart!
Was it to fling *this* at me that you came here?

Talleyrand.

Whenever I am damned for giving advice
I know that the advice will without doubt be
Taken. The Emperor says, " Damn you, Monsieur! "
And the next day the Emperor says, " Monsieur,
What do you think of such and such a plan, eh? "
My very plan. So then I say, " Not to be
Thought of, Sire! " The Emperor adopts it then.

Josephine.

(*Who has been pondering deeply.*)
Monsieur de Talleyrand.

Talleyrand.

Yours, Your Majesty.

Josephine.

Napoleon's child of whom you speak—his mother—

Talleyrand.

The mother would without a doubt be willing
To—to—to——

Josephine.

There is, then, something which Monsieur
Hesitates to say? I did not think there was.

Talleyrand.

Yes—some of the bishop hangs about me yet.

Josephine.

Some? Why, Monsieur de Talleyrand, the Bishop,
And our Monsieur de Talleyrand, the, the, the—

Talleyrand.

The pawn?

Josephine.

No, not the pawn; for pawns move on straight
Lines. What shall I say?—the knave!—

Talleyrand.

There are no knaves
In chess.

Josephine.

But in the game which we are playing?

Talleyrand.

All hangs upon one trick.

Josephine.

Which the knave can take?

Talleyrand.

No, not as against the queen; but with the queen,
Your Majesty—the queen and knave together.

Josephine.

You wish me to proclaim this bastard my child?[124]

Talleyrand.

Why not?   He is your husband's and, therefore, half
Your own.   The medical profession, doubtless,
Will certify that, contrary to all our
Fears, Your Majesty will be a mother soon.[125]

Josephine.

Experts have sworn that I cannot bear children.

Talleyrand.

Experts!   Your Majesty, there are more experts.

Nothing is easier than to find experts
Ready to swear to anything and *prove* it!

Josephine.

You tempt me, Talleyrand.   Yes, if the boy is
Born with eyes like his—oh!   God!

Talleyrand.
                        Your Majesty

Would own him for her child?   Then I can swear
   that
The divorce shall never more be spoken of.

Josephine.

But you forget one thing :—the—the mother!—

Talleyrand.
                       Bah !

She will agree to it to-night—joyfully.
    (*A very long pause.*)

Josephine.

I utterly deny it, and defy you !
No woman could do that and be a woman.
If this one should, the child whom she will bear
   would
Have the taint of her brute nature in his blood.
You brought me here to make that proposition?
Make it yourself !   And may the tigress, lurking
In mothers' hearts, spring from this outraged mother,
And rip and tear your blasted heart to pieces !
                            (*Exit.*

Talleyrand.

Fool! Fool! Fool! Fool! Then I must do it
    for you.

Rustan.

(*Starting up.*)
Rustan who never sleeps is here, Emperor!
    (NAPOLEON *is heard singing out of tune without.*)

Talleyrand.

The Emperor? That rascal Constant lied, then?
He must not find me here! Rustan, you black fiend!
    (*Enjoins silence on* RUSTAN, *and hides behind a
        table.*)
        Enter NAPOLEON.

Napoleon.

(*Singing lustily.*)
" *Out of myself! Out of myself!* "

Talleyrand.

(*Aside.*)
Out of his head? He owns to it at last, eh?

Napoleon.

(*Bellowing.*)
" *Out from myself:*
    Out from my past with its wrecks and contrition."
        Enter MME. WALEWSKA, *running.*

Mme. Walewska.

(*Taking up the song.*)
" *Come, come to me!* "
    (NAPOLEON *embraces her.*)

Talleyrand.

(*Aside.*)
Extremely pretty.

Napoleon.
You did not expect me?

Mme. Walewska.
Indeed, indeed, I did not!

Talleyrand.
(*Aside.*)   Neither did I!

Napoleon.
And the lover whom my jealousy told me
That I would find with you, is not here, is he?
Or have you hidden him behind the curtains?

Mme. Walewska.
You naughty, jealous sweetheart!   Look where you
    will.
If you can find a thing that has the slightest
Semblance to a man, or that could possibly
Be called a man, I'll own that I am fickle.

Talleyrand.
(*Aside.*)
This is becoming interesting—very!

Napoleon.
No, Marie, no, I will not look for him.

Talleyrand.

(*Aside.*) Thanks !

Napoleon.

I came to tell you what Monsieur Fouché says,
That devilish Monsieur de Talleyrand has
Hatched at last out of that hell he calls his heart.

Mme. Walewska.

Why do you drag that monster into our nest?
Would you allow him to come here in person ?

Napoleon.

If I should catch him here—but he knows better !
He is a good soul, too, in spite of all.   Why,
Do you know, that he is at this moment in
Very serious trouble owing to his
Devotion to us ?

Talleyrand.

(*Aside*). Don't mention it, please, Sire.

Mme. Walewska.

Well, drop his horrid name.

Talleyrand.

(*Aside*). Yes, change the subject.

Napoleon.

But I must tell you of his latest plotting.

Enter BABETTE *with a tray bearing chocolate. She
goes to table and discovers* TALLEYRAND, *who en-
joins silence.*

You see, Marie, he and Fouché are fencing.
Bring me my chocolate, Babette.   Talleyrand
Opposes the divorce—not that he cares a
Sou for Josephine—but to oppose Fouché.
    (*Drinks chocolate.*   BABETTE *returns to the table.*)

Babette.

(*Aside*).
Hello!

Talleyrand.

Sh—h !

Babette.

He won't hear you, and she won't tell.

Napoleon.

Another cup, Babette.   So then, as Fouché
Grows more vehement for the divorce, Monsieur
De Talleyrand cudgels his poor old empty
Pate for some deep scheme with which to circum-
    vent
His brother devil.   And what do you suppose
That he has hit upon ?

Talleyrand.

(*Aside.*)   This is delicious.

Mme. Walewska.

I can't imagine, Sire.

Napoleon.

Would you believe it?
He actually proposes to suggest
To you to sell your child to Josephine, who
Is to palm herself off as the mother.

Mme. Walewska.

(*Springs up.*)   What!
I am to sell my boy who is yours also?
I am to lie about the crowning glory
Of my life, and to deny, for pay, that I,
I, Marie Walewska, became the mother
Of Napoleon's boy? Where is the miscreant?
Is that the proposition which he intends
To make?
                    Talleyrand.
        (*Aside.*)
                Not now, I've changed my mind about it!

Babette.

Madame requires no further service?

Mme. Walewska.
                                            •   No, go!
        Babette.
(*To* Talleyrand.)
Now is your chance—only if Constant finds you!
        (*She takes the tray.* Talleyrand *hides behind her
            as she goes toward the door. Exeunt* Tal-
            leyrand *and* Babette.)

Napoleon.

Sit down, Sweetheart. I shall know how to colour
Your pale cheeks now, and not with rouge. I shall
   say,
Talleyrand!

Mme. Walewska.

      And all my blood will burn with shame
That such a monster should be called a man! Ugh!

Napoleon.

Away with thoughts of him! I came for peace,
   dear.
Love is that golden fact with which the heavy
Universe of man's anxiety and cares [126]
Is balanced—and out-weighed when balanced, leav-
   ing
The margin of preponderance on the side
Of joy! Life would not be worth living, nay, life
Could not at all be lived, but for love's mercy,
Which, with a measureless indifference to
Reason's dictates and to man's conventions, floods
All the world, and to each breaking heart unfolds
The incommunicable secret of one
Other heart, which is the answer and the end
Of the unutterable yearning of man's soul.

Mme. Walewska.

I love you so much more when you are sad, Sire.

Napoleon.

Then love me now as you have never loved me.

Mme. Walewska.

Are you so sad to-night, dear ? What makes you sad?

Napoleon.

Read this—it is from Josephine—and see !

Mme. Walewska.

(*Reads the note ; crumples it, falls at* NAPOLEON's
feet.)

Sire !

CURTAIN.

SCENE 2.—*A Gallery at Fontainebleau.*[127] *Morning.*

DISCOVERED—*A small table at centre front. Two
large chairs back to back near the table. In one
of them,* TALLEYRAND *sitting, in the other,* FOUCHÉ.
After a sullen silence.

Talleyrand.

Monsieur Fouché puts on as many airs as
If his own scheme for divorce had done so much !

Fouché.

Monsieur de Talleyrand is naturally sore,
Since his fine scheme for—what would you call your
scheme—

Oh! yes—since his fine scheme for cheating nature
And making the barren bear, has come to naught.

Talleyrand.

When his own scheme has carried, Monsieur Fouché
May laugh : till then let him not brag of what he
Will, or will not, do with these women.   Burn them !

Fouché.

Ha! ha! ha! ha!   Were they so very dreadful ?
The rumour is, that Monsieur de Talleyrand
Was so unmercifully trounced on making
His gallant proposition to madame wife,
That he was glad enough to drop the matter
And get away alive without so much as
Mentioning the bargain to madame mistress !

Talleyrand.

They lie, Monsieur Fouché.   I saw my errour,
And so desisted and instantly withdrew.

Fouché.

Behind the petticoat of fair Babette, eh ?

Talleyrand.

Another arrant lie !   Monsieur Fouché, I
Do confess that I am guilty of a crime.

Fouché.

(*Turning his chair partly around.*)

It was much worse than a mere crime, it was a
blunder ! [128]

Talleyrand.

Spoken like a true politician.
It was a blunder.   Crimes can be forgiven.

Fouché.

But blunders never !   Monsieur de Talleyrand
Has but one way in which to overtake this
Terrible mistake and regain ground.

Talleyrand.
(*Turning his chair partly around.*)
What way ?

Fouché.
By helping me.

Talleyrand.
To compass the—

Fouché.
The divorce.

Talleyrand.
You never can break down Napoleon's scruples.

Fouché.
He never in his life had one of those things !

Talleyrand.
Not against breaking the commandments, Fouché,
No one in these days has ; but Bonaparte is
Scrupulous to a degree about having
His own way !

Fouché.

Then you must make his way our way.

Talleyrand.

Have you not tried to?

Fouché.

    Monsieur de Talleyrand
Has not; until he has, we must not lose heart.

Talleyrand.

(*Aside.*)
There must be something back of this; what is it?
 (*Aloud.*)
Monsieur Fouché is very generous, but
He allows his manners to blind his reason.
What arguments, in heaven's name, could I make
Use of that have not long ago occurred to
One whose fund of arguments in this respect
Is inexhaustible?

Fouché.

    Monsieur forgets one
Most important fact. Monsieur de Talleyrand
Has until now been bitterly opposed to
The divorce. Now, don't Monsieur observe that, if
 (*He hitches his chair completely around.*)
Monsieur suddenly turns around and favours
The divorce, he will have influence beyond
All mine? Commend me to a convert always

For telling arguments, for truth sits lightly
On those who hold to it by being born to't.
Till now Monsieur de Talleyrand has always
Pulled one way, and I the other ; and neither
Moved an inch one way or the other.   Now let
Us pull together and results will follow.

(TALLEYRAND *wheels his chair around.*)

Talleyrand.

But Josephine !

Fouché.
Oh, I'll manage her.

Talleyrand.

Perhaps.
Fouché.
I never found the woman yet I could not.

Talleyrand.
Well, if you want to make that record stand you,
Take my advice, and never ask a mother
To disown her child.

Fouché.
Nor to give birth to one
By proxy ?   No, I shall not.

Talleyrand.
A mother is
A riddle I give up.   Nothing corrupts her.
The woman who will sell her soul, and argue

Like a man, and barter this and that, for her
Advantage, becomes unreasonably pure,
Ineffably unselfish, stupidly great,
The moment that you do but mention her child.

Fouché.

No fear that I shall meddle much with mothers.

Talleyrand.

Be wise, and do not.

Fouché.

    If you will bolster up
Napoleon's courage, I will fix—Josephine.
The Emperor has given me permission
To open fire, and Josephine will be here
In a moment ; but he is so insanely
Superstitious, that he may even yet spoil
Everything, if she begins to roll her
Eyes up at him and call herself his star.[12]

Talleyrand.

          Bah !
We shall eclipse this star.

Fouché.

    For this eclipsing
I am your man ; for I am nothing, if not
Opaque.   Now, if Monsieur de Talleyrand will
Guarantee to keep his Majesty, the sun,
Shining in one fixed place for the next half-hour,

I pledge my soul on totally eclipsing
This star of destiny.   I hear her coming.

Talleyrand.

Then to my work.   Where can I find Napoleon ?

Fouché.

(*Accompanying* TALLEYRAND *to door.*)

· Biting his nails, I guess, out on the terrace.
Sweep him before you like a broken mill-dam !
Say France, France, France, every five minutes, and
Ask him, in between, whom he prefers, Bourbons
Or nephews, to succeed him ?   Then send him in.
I think that the eclipse will become total
In fifteen minutes.   Yes, send him in to her
In fifteen minutes.   Quick !   Here she is !

Talleyrand.

Till then——
And, Fouché, say a good word for me, will you ?
(*Exit* TALLEYRAND.

Enter JOSEPHINE.

Josephine.

The Emperor has sent me this—look at it.
(*Hands* FOUCHÉ *a note.*)
Monsieur Fouché desires to consult with us.
Monsieur Fouché has the permission of the
Emperor.   Will, then, Monsieur Fouché please have
The goodness to come immediately and

Without ceremony to the important
Question which seems to trouble Monsieur Fouché?

Fouché.

Say, rather, France, your Majesty—which troubles
France. The question of all questions which threatens
France with grave confusion till it be settled. [130]

Josephine.

Affairs of state would best be settled by those
To whom the government has been entrusted.

Fouché.

Certain affairs of state, however, require
Your Majesty's attention, because they do
More nearly touch herself.

Josephine.

      What! Monsieur Fouché,
Monsieur Fouché! You are an arrant coward.
By some foul lie you have induced the kindness
Of my husband to grant you this disgraceful
Opportunity to once again insult
Me. I see your devilish heart, you monster!
You mean divorce! That is the precious question
Which requires all this mysterious cringing
At my heels, this fawning, this palavering,
These lies! Have you forgotten, fiend, what treat-
    ment
You received from your imperial master
When you presumed to meddle with my honour?

Fouché.

That was two years ago, your Majesty.

Josephine.

Well?

Well? What if it were two hundred years ago?
Have I grown less his wife? Does marriage loosen
With the lapse of time? Monsieur Fouché will not
Expect to find me willing to hear one word
From him or any other man, except my
Husband, upon the question of my divorce!

Fouché.

In what I was about to say, believe me,
It was His Majesty's own pleasure I meant
To serve. He sent me here.

Josephine.

That is a black lie.

Fouché.

Let his own hand attest it. Be pleased to read.
    (JOSEPHINE *reads the note authorizing* FOUCHÉ *to
       propose the divorce. Paralyzed with horror
       she sinks upon a chair.*)
Your Majesty will hear me now, I dare say?

Josephine.

Say on.

Fouché.

The arguments by which—

Josephine.

Don't argue.

Fouché.

There is no need of it, in truth, for one word,
France, is the whole argument.   Your Majesty,
If this divorce were planned in order to make
Room for some mere wanton favourite—not an
Unheard of thing either with kings—I pledge you
That I would oppose any such outrage, yes,
At the cost of life.

Josephine.

Go on!   Go on!   Monsieur.
Who would have dreamed of such devotion to us?

Fouché.

Or if there were the faintest hope of Heaven's
Blessing your Majesty with children, why then,
Whoever breathed a syllable looking to
A divorce, were guilty of high treason.

Josephine.

Thanks.

Fouché.

And as for these nefarious suggestions
Of palming off some favourite's bastard son

As the legitimate and lawful offspring
Of Your Majesty—the very thought is such
As no one but a miscreant could entertain.

Josephine.

Like Talleyrand.

Fouché.

                Thank providence, one does not
Have to apologize for what that man does !

Josephine.

Monsieur Fouché has shown to us on what grounds
It would have been impossible for him to
Advocate the sacrilege and outrage which
He has sought this interview to urge.   There are,
No doubt, grounds upon which even his tender
Conscience and deep devotion feel justified
In doing so.   Will he proceed ?   Begin—" but "—

Fouché.

But when one thinks of France, and that the Em-
    pire,
So marvellously reared by the resistless
Armies of the Man of Destiny, stands now
Upon no broader basis than his one life,
A life so constantly exposed to dangers,
Who does not join his sighs to those which have
    been
Wrung from Your Majesty over the failure
Of providence, in its mysterious ways,
To bless your marriage?

Josephine.

(*Rising.*)   Where is the Emperor?

Fouché.

Close by, Your Majesty, upon the terrace.

Josephine.

When he has found the Emperor and told him
That we especially desire his presence,
Monsieur Fouché will go and never, if he
Values his own peace, disturb ours more.   Begone!

Fouché.

With one word of assurance that France may look—

Josephine.

Take the assurance, then, Monsieur Fouché, that
France will never have a truer friend than I.
                    (*Exit* Fouché.
Oh!   Heaven grant me grace to be a good wife!

Enter Napoleon.   *A long silence.*

Napoleon.

Have you no argument but tears?

Josephine.
                    One other:
I am your wife.[131]

Napoleon.
                    Must we begin so far back?

Josephine.

We must end there.   Wherever we may begin.

Napoleon.

And drown the hopes of France in tears?   Just like
      you !

Josephine.

I promise not to cry.

Napoleon.

                  Make no such promise,
Josephine, unless you are prepared to make
The pitiless sacrifice which France demands.
If you are not prepared ; if Monsieur Fouché's
Arguments have not convinced you ; if you still
See some way to the establishment of our
Empire upon a sure foundation without
The terrible necessity of this which
Racks my soul ; for my sake, Josephine, reserve
Your argument of tears ; for against your tears
I never could and never shall contend.[132]

Josephine.

                        Oh !

Sire, I thank you for those words, and you will see
That, notwithstanding that I have such power,
I will not by so much as one salt tear, stand
Between you and glory.   I am convinced now.
I am prepared to make the sacrifice which
France—our France—demands.

Napoleon.

It is indeed our France.
Your France no less than mine. I gained the battles,[133]
But you won men's hearts, and so together we
Built up this France which now demands this awful
Token of our boundless love.

Josephine.

Assure me first
That what I hear is false. They say some mistress—

Napoleon.

They lie, whoever they may be! Some mistress!
Shame, Josephine. You're jealousy incarnate![134]

Josephine.

If I have been the body, as you declare,
Of jealousy, you have been jealousy's own
Spirit making me live. Jealous! Good heavens!
What woman would have been insulted as I
Have, and not been jealous? And as for that, have
You not heaped upon my head, time after time,
The most outrageous charges which jealousy[135]
Run mad could hatch? The time has come for speaking.

Napoleon.

Well, then, the time has come for both of us to
Speak. I could have stood your preaching, Josephine,

Had you been one whit less unfaithful than I
Have been.   As God is witness, I was not false
Until I could no longer doubt my senses
And knew you to have been unfaithful to me.[136]

Josephine.

It is a damnable falsehood, straight from hell !
Name him, Napoleon.   Name just one man for whom
I, even in my heart, have felt what should have
Been felt only for yourself.   Don't turn it off !
If you can name him, do so !

Napoleon.

                    Well, then, I will.
But why be so particular about it ?
In Egypt, Germany, Italy, and Spain,
Wherever I was fighting, my heart was wrung
By the incessant tidings of your amours.[137]

Josephine.

Rumours which to an absent lover always
Seem black.   Confess that you cannot name one man.

Napoleon.

I can !   Out of a score that I could name you,
I name you Monsieur Charles !   Come, now, what
     say you ?[138]
     (JOSEPHINE *not expecting this, betrays confusion.*)
Forgive me, Josephine.   I did not mean to
Resurrect, in this our last hour, those bitter
Criminations and recriminations which

Have already done so much toward wrecking
A life that might have been, beyond words, peaceful.

Josephine.

I have in every point endeavoured, Sire,
To be a good wife.

Napoleon.

      And you have succeeded.
How to go out into the future, darling,
Without you, is the question which fills my heart
With inexpressible distress and anguish.

Josephine.

And it must be?

Napoleon.

      If France is to continue
After my death.

Josephine.

      And this div——

(*Sobs.*)

Napoleon.

          Tears, Josephine?

Josephine.

No! No! I will be true! Have you decided
When I am to—when the divorce—Napoleon!

Napoleon.

It will be best to consummate the matter
Without delay.

Josephine.

Yes!   What would you call delay?

Napoleon.

Ten days, or so—at the outside, a fortnight.[139]

Josephine.

Good God! forgive me, I am not very well,
May this last hour be all mine, all mine, husband?

Napoleon.

All yours, all yours, dear, as I shall ever be.

Josephine.

And you will not be angry with me, will you?
And I may feel as if this were our first, and
Not our last hour, and that an everlasting
Joy was just beginning, not the eternal
Darkness that has begun?

Napoleon.

Yes, Josephine, but
For the sake of France, do not pretend this joy
Too skilfully, lest we lay hands upon it,
And make it stay, and drive that nightmare, duty,
Away forever.   I love you, Josephine.

Josephine.

And when I am divorced, whom will you marry?[140]

Napoleon.

Hush! You will break my heart! Some woman,
    doubtless.

Josephine.

God! If it only might be some man, some man,
But not a woman! You do not know just what
An agony a woman feels, Napoleon,
At the bare thought of having any other
Woman in her place. And—and this is my place.

Napoleon.

And where you are no other ever can be.
You were made mine not by a ceremony,
But by that Destiny which has forever [141]
Set me apart from other men, above them.
I am no ordinary man, nor am I
Bound by ordinary laws of morals, or [142]
Of life. The sooner that the world discovers
This, the better! And Josephine, Destiny
Laid its irresistible decrees on you,
And you are bound inextricably to me.
Think not, therefore, that any separation
Is separation, nor that divorce will mean
Divorce of soul.

Josephine.

        Sublime, but keep such comforts
For the dark hours that are to come to-morrow.
This hour is mine, a simple human woman,
And neither thoughts of Destiny, nor sublime

Metaphors can stop the ache here in my heart.
Before I have to face that awful future ;
Before I have to brace myself to leave you ;
Before I hear your marriage bells ring,
And am compelled to learn your new wife's name,
    oh !
Let me live again the past with you ! Do ! Do !
    (*She rings a table-bell.*)

Napoleon.

But without witnesses, I beg you.

Enter a SERVANT.

Josephine.
                Pray bid
Madame de Rémusat to come here quickly.
                      (*Exit* SERVANT.
Yes, without witnesses. Upon our sorrows
All the world may stare, but on a wife's sweet past
It would be sacrilege for anyone to
Look, except her husband.

Enter MME. DE RÉMUSAT.

                My letter casket,
Bring it to me, dear.

Mme. de Rémusat.
              At once, Your Majesty.
             (*Exit* MME. DE RÉMUSAT.

Napoleon.

Will this not prove too painful?

Josephine.

Painful! Your love?

Napoleon.

The past makes even happiness seem sad.

Josephine.

True,

But when one has no future the past means all.

Napoleon.

This is your hour, poor child.

Josephine.

Then let me fill it,

Up to the very brim with your old dear self.

Enter Mme. de Rémusat *with the casket.*

Here, give it me, Clari.

Mme. de Rémusat.

And then?

Josephine.

Then go, dear,

(Mme. de Rémusat *goes to the door; returns,*
falls at Napoleon's *feet imploringly, cannot*
speak, exit, hastily.)

Napoleon.

(*Pacing about the room.*)
Poor France!   At this rate how can we persevere?

Josephine.

(*Having opened the casket and untied the letters,
          reads aloud.*)
"But I am sure that you will always be my
Faithful consort, as I shall be your fondest
Lover.   Yes, death alone can break the union
Which sympathy and love and sentiment have
Formed."   You wrote that in the hour of glory—[143]

Napoleon.

                                        Where?

Josephine.

Verona, upon the twenty-ninth, at noon.

Napoleon.

Verona?   That was immediately, then,
After Arcola.

Josephine.

                        Your letter glows with news
Of Arcola—and love for me.

Napoleon.

                              Arcola!
Arcola!   Read no more, Josephine, no more.
       (*To himself.*)
We took five thousand prisoners and killed at

Least six thousand of the enemy.   But for
The blunder of Vaubois in abandoning
Rivoli, we might have———[114]

Josephine.

Here is another :
(*Reads.*)
" There is only one woman for me.   Do you
Know her?   If I should draw her portrait, you would
Not recognize it, Josephine, thinking it
Flattery. . . . I find the nights so very long
In solitude.   I love you—long so for you." [115]

Napoleon.

Be merciful to me ; if you must read, read
To yourself.   I cannot stand it.   Where was I
When I wrote that letter?

Josephine.

At Posen.

Napoleon.

Posen ! [116]

Josephine.

Posen !   You start.   Does memory accuse you?

Napoleon.

That was a hard and memorable winter.
(*Aside.*)
Marie Walewska was in my arms that night.
(*Aloud.*)
Be merciful.   Shut up the casket, won't you?

Josephine.

This is my hour.   And I would have you once more
Mine altogether as these old lines prove you.
      (*Reads.*)   .
"My only Josephine, away from you there
Is no happiness ; the world a desert where
I stand alone.   My hand is on my heart ; your
Image beats there, I look at it, and love is
Perfect happiness for me." [117]

Napoleon.

                        Josephine, stop !

Josephine.

      (*Reads on.*)
"To live for Josephine.   That is the story
Of my life."

Napoleon.

      (*Snatching the letters.*)
                  You shall not torture me like that !

Josephine.

      (*Getting another letter from the casket.*)
It is my hour, Napoleon—it is my last.
This looks to be a very old one—then it
Is surely sweet.   Wives must look far, far backward
To find their lovers.   Yes, it is very old ;
You wrote it, husband, in Italy in June ;
How sweet it must be !   We had just been married.

Napoleon.

(*Taking her in his arms.*)
You shall not read it ; I shall block the way
Before each word with kisses.   Give it to me.

Josephine.

Let me read just this one, written in June in
Italy—the sky, the flowers are in it.[18]
    (*Reads.*)
" A thousand kisses on your eyes, your lips.   Oh !
What a great power you have over me, my
Queen ! "   What is this ?   Napoleon, for God's sake,
    look !

Napoleon.

(*Taking the letter.*)
Where ?   I see naught but love, love, love.

Josephine.

                                    All love, but
With what awful meaning in it now.   Look at
That sentence.   Look !

Napoleon.

(*Reads.*)   " A child as lovely as its
Mother will be born to you."   You must not read !
    (*Throws down letter.*)

Josephine.

(*Picking up letter and kissing it.*)
It never, never, came, that little child !

Napoleon.

Stop !

Josephine.

He never came to save his mother from this
Hour of shame.

Napoleon.

It is enough ! You are my wife,
And while I live you shall not be an outcast.
     (IMPERATOR *glides in while* NAPOLEON *speaks and
          remains unobserved at rear.*)
And what is life at all, but a blind groping,
A thirst, a feverish pursuit, a death-throe ?
The glory that lures men on hovers above
Destruction ; and while they listen to the lies
Which Destiny and Fate seduce them with, Life,
Deep, warm, honest, humble life, lies in their grasp !
We press toward the attainment of our dreams
Trampling realities beneath our feet ! No !
I have dreamed enough ! Destiny shall no more
Cheat me of what I have by promises of
What I might have, Josephine, I swear by—Look ! [149]
     (*He catches sight of* IMPERATOR *who menaces.*)

Josephine.

Is some one near us ? You are as white and cold
As if you had again seen Charlemagne.

Napoleon.

Hush!
I had forgotten France in thinking only
Of ourself.   It must be, Josephine!   Divorce!

Josephine.

(*Falls at his feet.*)
No!   No!   Not after what you have been saying—
Napoleon, look at me!   Don't stare so ghastly
At that hallucination of your brain.   Look!
Look at me.   I am your fact, your actual peace,
Whatever your ambition may tempt you with.

Napoleon.

(*Gazing fixedly at* IMPERATOR.)
Up, Josephine, get up!   Will you desert me
At an hour like this?   The destinies of France
Hang in the balance of your favour, woman,
And for a kiss you will betray your trust?

Josephine.

(*Rises.*)   No!
True to myself by being true to you, I [130]
Shall prove true to France.   Proclaim me not your
    wife.
(IMPERATOR *vehemently commands compliance.*)

Napoleon.

I cannot, Josephine.   You are my wife—but

Yes, it must be. I am the man the Empire,
France, the universe, require. I follow thee.
   (*To* Imperator, *who goes out.*)

        Josephine.

(*Gathering the scattered letters.*)
My hour is past. Tell me that I have been a
Good wife to you.

        Napoleon.

     History, Josephine, to
The remotest ages will celebrate you.
Adieu! Adieu! Adieu! indissolubly
Mine in soul. The time has come now when you
    must
Formally announce your willingness. A line
Will do; I may expect it from you shortly?

        Josephine.

At once! At once! I cannot promise to be
Strong to-morrow. What shall I write, my hus-
    band?

        Napoleon.

Two words — your bare consent. You have no
    paper?

        Josephine.

Yes. Let me write on this—the back of this dear
Note, written in June in Italy—the one
In which you speak about the child that never—
   (*Breaks down.*)

Napoleon.

Sacrilege, no !

Josephine.

Sanctification, rather !
Yes, it must be on this, then God will bless it.
(*She writes, then reads aloud.*)
" The Empress heartily accords in feeling
With the Emperor, that the best interests
Of France require that she be now divorced, to
The intent that — to the intent that — that —
that——" [151]

Napoleon.

(*Taking the paper out of her hand.*)
Stop, Josephine! Stop, Josephine, I cannot
Bear this strain—something is tearing me. Adieu.

Josephine.

My husband—tell me—I am a good wife.

Napoleon.

God !

(NAPOLEON *goes slowly to the door, there he turns.*
JOSEPHINE *stretches her arms to him, chok-*
ing. He goes out frantic. JOSEPHINE
swoons.) [152]

CURTAIN.

ACT IV.

THE SHADOW OF DEATH.—1814.

ACT IV.

SCENE 1.—*A Bed room at Malmaison.*[153] *Night.*

DISCOVERED—JOSEPHINE *lying upon a lounge,* HOR-
TENSE *bending over her.* COUNTESS WALEWSKA
softly fingering her lute at side.

Josephine.

(*In great weakness.*)
Who came while I was sleeping? Tell me, Hortense.

Hortense.

Only Marie, Mamma. [154]

Josephine.

    I heard a man's voice.
I dreamed about the Emperor. It seemed that
He was in some awful peril, and that he
Sent to me, to Josephine, his wife, for help! [155]

Hortense.

It was the Duke's voice.

Josephine.

   The Duke's? What Duke, Hortense?
How can you all be so unmerciful? God!

He is in peril—Napoleon in peril ! [156]
And you will not so much as tell me what has
Befallen him !   Who came ?   What duke has been
     here ?

Hortense.

Only the Duke of Vicenza. [157]

Josephine.

                                   Caulaincourt ?
What has brought him to Paris ?   Hark !   What
     was that ?
Did you not hear the roar of cannon ?   Paris
Is lost.   Help !   Help !   Help there !   Paris is
     taken !
     (*Struggles to her feet.*)

Mme. Walewska.

(*Coming to aid* HORTENSE.)
It was my lute.   I played a battle song.

Josephine.

                                        No !
The Emperor is taken !   I am his star !
My heart has cracked—look, look ! from the top to
     the
Bottom !   And it has paralyzed Napoleon's
Great right arm.   But where is he ?   In just what
     shape
Has this inevitable ruin perched upon

His eagles? Away from me! Hortense! Marie!
The Empress of the French—make way there for us!
  (*Falls fainting.*)

Mme. Walewska.

In very mercy, let us tell her, Hortense.

Hortense.

I am her child, I cannot——

Mme. Walewska.

                    And I am more.
I am the mortal enemy who triumphed
Over her, robbed her of peace, drove red-hot
Evidences of my success into her
Broken heart: I am the woman whom she could
Single out to curse—and she forgave me! Yes,
Took me to share with her that outcast life, which
Is the price all pay who love ingratitude.

Hortense.

But we must tell her. This terrible suspense
Will injure her. You see that it is useless
To try to overcome her fears with reasons.

Mme. Walewska.

She sleeps more calmly now——

Hortense.

                    Good! turn down the light

Marie, and bring your lute.   Sing for good dreams
now.
(MME. WALEWSKA *hums very softly.*)

Josephine.
(*Brokenly in her sleep.*)
          That was a lie they told the Emperor!

Hortense.
(*Softly to* MME. WALEWSKA.)
                                        Sing!

Josephine.
They told him that his Josephine was dead.

Hortense.
                              Sing!
Josephine.
And he could fight no more.

Hortense.
                    Sing, sing!

Mme. Walewska.
(*Tries, sobs, breaks down.*)   I cannot!

Josephine.
(*Rousing herself partially.*)
I see Napoleon standing upon a rock ;
The dreary, heartless sea surges around him.
He is alone, disgraced—look! look! look!
     (*Falls back.*)

Hortense.

It was
A dream—only a dream, Mamma.

Mme. Walewska.

Josephine !

Josephine.

Where is Marie?   Give me your hand, Marie, so ;
Now look, see where I point—you should be able
To see him as I do, because you also
Have felt his heart beat—can you not see him ?
  Look !

Hortense.

(*To* MME. WALEWSKA.)
I cannot bear this, Marie.   Sing, for God's sake.

Mme. Walewska.

(*Clinging to* JOSEPHINE.)
Indeed, indeed, I do not see him, darling.

Josephine.

Of course not !   And, pray, why should you ?

Mme. Walewska.

You said so.

Josephine.

What did I say ?   I deny it.   I said that—
  (*Struggles to get up.*)
You shall NOT keep me !   Look !   He beckons to me.
If he would only look this way !   Napoleon !

Your Majesty! My husband! Look, it is I.
It is your Josephine. She is not dead, no!
She is quite well, and strong, and coming to you!
Strike! Strike your enemies back into the dust!
As long as I live, you are the Emperor
Invincible—and I do live! Josephine!
(*Rises triumphantly.*)

Enter CAULAINCOURT.

Hortense.

Your Grace observes now that the end is coming.

Caulaincourt.

The end has come. Paris is in the hands of
The Allied Powers.[15]

Hortense.

The Emperor, your Grace?

Caulaincourt.

(*Greatly moved, and with hesitation.*)
The Emperor—The Emperor——

Josephine.

(*Noticing* CAULAINCOURT's *presence.*)
Caulaincourt,
Come to us. Someone has lied. Someone has told
The Emperor that I am dead. I am not!
Go, Caulaincourt, go now, go now, before it
Is too late. Tell him that Josephine will come
With reinforcements—more than a million men!

Caulaincourt.

(*To* HORTENSE.)
Shall I inform her Majesty?

Hortense.
I beg you.

Caulaincourt.

(*Kneeling.*)
Your Majesty.

Josephine.
Not gone yet, Caulaincourt? Go!

Caulaincourt.

I went and have returned. The Emperor sends
His devoted heart——

Josephine.
Where is the Emperor?

Caulaincourt.

At Fontainebleau.[159]

Josephine.
At Fontainebleau? He is well?

Caulaincourt.

The Emperor is well. He has surrendered.[160]

Josephine.

(*Springing to her feet.*)

Surrendered! When did the end come, Caulaincourt?

Caulaincourt.

This morning.

Josephine.

The hour?

Caulaincourt.

At dawn, your Majesty!

Josephine.

Hortense, I died at dawn this morning. Inform
The Court.

(*Sinks in deep thought.*)

Go, Caulaincourt. Go, Hortense, also.
Marie and I alone must pass beyond this.
The Emperor is gathering his last Court:
They only enter there who loved him truly.
Marie, play on your lute, child, as they go out.

(*Exeunt* HORTENSE *and* CAULAINCOURT, *slowly.*
Now to our glorious privilege, Marie.

(*Supported by* MME. WALEWSKA, JOSEPHINE *crosses
to a curtained recess, where they kneel and
pray before an oratory.*)

CURTAIN.

Scene 2.—*A Bed-room at Fontainebleau.*[161]

Discovered—Napoleon, *haggard and dishevelled, sitting in an arm-chair before the fire. A small mahogany table. A little yellow sofa. A window with balcony at rear.* Rustan *standing at the door. After a pause, enter* Macdonald. [162]

Macdonald.

Sire.

Napoleon.

Macdonald?

Macdonald.

Sign—if you wish to live, Sire.[163]
(*Offers the abdication to* Napoleon.)

Napoleon.

(*Crumpling the paper and throwing it away.*)
How say you? If I wish to live? They threaten?

Macdonald.

Sire, nothing but abdication can now save
France. My brother Marshals and myself have spent
All day in fruitless efforts to avert this.[164]

Napoleon.

You are a pack of cowards, traitors, women!

Macdonald.

Sire, if you had heard the sobs which broke from
us—

Napoleon.

True, dear Macdonald, true.   You are no coward!
You crossed the Splugen and forced your way into
The Valteline, when Hannibal himself would
Have declared the feat impossible.   Do not
Imagine, man, that I forget such triumphs.
But, in the name of France and of our eagles,
Why may we not yet rally? [105]

Macdonald.
                   Impossible!

Napoleon.

You lie, Macdonald, or you keep back the facts.
Paris is in the hands of Russians.   All France
Is filled with the in-pouring enemies of
Her Imperial head—the Allies number [106]
More than twice our force.   What of it?   It is not
The first time that you and I have had to face
Superior numbers, nor must you surely
Have to be told so late, that with one Frenchman
A dozen other soldiers are off-set.   No!
This is outrageous!   Macdonald, summon a
Council of our Marshals instantly!   Hear me?
If they so much as hesitate, order them
Shot!   Wounds!   Malediction!   The streets of Paris
Swarming with Prussian thieves, and we, we, we! the
Conqueror of Europe, here at Fontainebleau
With tens of thousands of our loyal soldiers,
Armed, eager, thirsting for the word—I say, we

Lie here mocked by a horde of poltroon Marshals!
Macdonald, summon no Council of poltroons.
Order the second Corps to move on Paris![167]
Caulaincourt will join Ney at once, while your own
Troops will fall back on the Seine above——

Macdonald.

But, Sire!

Napoleon.

Not one word, traitor. Do you defy us? Go!

Macdonald.

With my last breath I will defend you, Sire. Your
Orders—

Napoleon.

Marmont will—

Macdonald.

But, Sire, the forces of [168]
Marmont are lost. Marmont has recognized the
Government.

Napoleon.

Villain! Then let Berthier advance——

Macdonald.

Alas! Sire, the Prince de Neufchatel also
Has just submitted to the Provisional
Government at Paris—[169]

Napoleon.

Berthier? Not Berthier?
Oh! Mankind! Mankind! Macdonald, yesterday,[170]

Yesterday, I say, Berthier was here with me.
He put his arms about me, and dwelt upon
The test which times like these are upon friendship.
Yes, he, Berthier, Berthier, whom I made Prince
    and [171]
Marshal! Bade me farewell as tenderly as
One who leaves the mistress of his soul. Berthier!
    (*Falls into the chair.*)

Macdonald.

The Emperor has other orders?

Napoleon.

                      No! No!

Macdonald.

Have I permission, then, to state the facts?

Napoleon.

                      Yes.

Macdonald.

All might have been averted, had but the King
Of Naples not played so falsely.[172]

Napoleon.

                 That is my
Sister's work. Caroline, I curse you! Go on! [173]

Macdonald.

The failure of his thirty thousand soldiers,
On whom depended——[174]

Napoleon.

I know all that.   Read me
No lecture, man.   Of Paris now, and this new
Government which the accursèd populace
Has bowed to—tell me of that !   Tell me of that !

Macdonald.

Monsieur de Talleyrand is at the forefront
Of it—[175]

Napoleon.

If there were any hot enough hell,
I would say damn Talleyrand eternally !

Macdonald.

All of Your Majesty's ministers have gone,
Fouché has gone.[176]

Napoleon.

Fouché !   Fouché, Fouché—fiend !

Macdonald.

The household, the civil service to a man,
Society—all Paris is proclaiming
Louis the Eighteenth ! [177]

Napoleon.

(*Starting up.*)   Macdonald, in God's name !

Macdonald.

Nothing can possibly prevent the Bourbons
From returning but instant abdication !

Napoleon.

Then it must be, Macdonald.   I abdicate.[178]

Macdonald.

(*Falling upon his knees.*)
Sire, it is at this supremest moment that
Your Imperial Majesty is thrice crowned![179]
I hasten to advise the anxious Marshals,
That our adored Commander has determined now
To add the star of sacrifice and mercy
To the immortal lustre of his crown.

Napoleon.

Go.
(*Exit* MACDONALD.

Rustan, tell Constant to come here and quickly.
(*Exit* RUSTAN.

A little while—or years—what can it matter?[180]
In politics there is no resurrection.[181]
In war, defeat is but the prelude and the
Discipline before success.   In love—why, love
Itself consists of vacillation and of
Failures, surviving all catastrophes, save
The one fatal danger of calm possession.
But he who falls from favour with the people
Has fallen forever!   The people never
Laugh at puppets after they have caught sight once
Of the trickery of wire-pulling by which
They are moved!   The people welcome mounte-
banks

But once. This blast has blown aside my curtains!
The people have now seen their idol naked.
In politics there is no resurrection.

Enter CONSTANT *and* RUSTAN.

Constant.

To serve you, Sire——

Napoleon.

Constant, where is the poniard?

Constant.

What poniard, Sire? [182]

Napoleon.

Why, the Arabian poniard,
Blockhead, which I commanded you to leave here.

Constant.

It was so dull that I had taken it, Sire,
To have it edged——

Napoleon.

Bring it at once, and next time
Sharpen your wits instead. Where are my pistols?

Constant.

Here, Sire, upon the table.

Napoleon.

Load them and go!
(*Exit* CONSTANT—*returns with the poniard.*

(CONSTANT *goes toward the door.*)
Constant !

Constant.

Sire ?

Napoleon.

Your house is not in good repair?

Constant.

Falling to pieces, Sire.

Napoleon.

(*Musing.*)   Like mine, Constant.

Constant.

Sire ?

Napoleon.

You will receive the sum of fifty thousand
Francs— [183]

Constant.

This terrifies me, Sire ; what does it mean ?

Napoleon.

You are forgetting to load the pistols now :
Load them and go. Has no word yet arrived from
Malmaison ?

(CONSTANT *loads the pistols.*)

Constant.

No word has come as yet, Sire.

Napoleon.

Go!

(*Exit* CONSTANT.

Rustan.

Rustan hears danger! Rustan hears woman's step!

Napoleon.

If it be she of whom we spoke, admit her.
    (*A knock is heard.*)
Rustan, obey me! Admit her instantly.
    (RUSTAN *opens the door, through which* MME.
        WALEWSKA, *closely veiled, rushes to* NAPO-
        LEON.)
Marie! At last! At last! I had begun to
Think that you had failed me as the rest all have.

Mme. Walewska.

I can remain a moment only, Sire, and
From that moment I must keep all myself out;
It is of Josephine that I have come to
Speak. This moment, I am told, may be our last
Together, heart of my heart, life of my soul;
But I must not speak of myself—don't make me!

Napoleon.

Speak as you will, I care not since you are here.
    (*In his arms.*)
Of Josephine—yes, speak of her. She is well?

Mme. Walewska.

You had not heard ?   She is dying, Sire——

Napoleon.

Good God !

Mme. Walewska.

She has been failing for two months——

Napoleon.

Exactly

The same time that fortune fled from my armies.[184]

Mme. Walewska.

Two days ago she utterly gave up ——

Napoleon.

Just

At the moment that the capital of France
Was taken.

Mme. Walewska.

To-day she hovers between life [185]
And death.   She will not live to see the sun set.

Napoleon.

Then before sunset I shall have fallen too.
And how in this last hour of it, does my poor
Josephine comport herself ?

Mme. Walewska.

Unspeakably,

Majestically ; so sweet ! so womanly !

And, Sire, to the last labouring heart-beat she
Is yours!

Napoleon.

Go to her—go at once—go madly!
And fill up these remaining moments of her
Grief with my repentant and devoted tears.
Go! Go! And tell Josephine, my star, that I
Am true to her in destiny, and that when
She to-day breaks from this cursèd prison-house
To throw herself upon the rest eternal,
Tell her, that at that moment will the Empire
Fall, and I be trampled in the dust of death.
Go, Marie, go, without another word. Go!

    (MME. WALEWSKA *goes to the door—returns—*
       hangs convulsively upon NAPOLEON, *and then*
       hurriedly exit.)

Enter CAULAINCOURT.

Caulaincourt.

Worthier lips than mine have told you all, Sire?

Napoleon.

Give me a moment's peace, Caulaincourt, can't you?
Forgive me. You were at Malmaison. You know.
No wonder that all efforts proved so futile!
You saw her: she is dying—she—Caulaincourt,
Josephine is ——

Enter MACDONALD *and* NEY.

    Macdonald, Ney,—you have heard?

Ney.

Yes, Sire.   You are now prepared to abdicate?

Napoleon.

Anything—Josephine is dying.—My pen !
(*Finds that he cannot write legibly.*)
I cannot write my own humiliation.
Macdonald, Ney, one of you write it for me.
(*Macdonald prepares to write—waits.*)
Go on !   Go on !

Macdonald.

But what to say, Sire—the words ?

Napoleon.

Give me the pen !   I cannot dictate my shame. [186]
(*Sits and writes rapidly, throws paper toward*
NEY.)
Read it, Ney, read !

Ney.

(*Reads.*)   "The Allied Powers having
Declared that the Emperor Napoleon is
The only obstacle—"
(*Breaks down.*)

Macdonald.

Permit us, Sire, to read
It one by one silently.
(*Reads.*)   Here, Caulaincourt.
(CAULAINCOURT *reads it—then* NEY—*all shake their*
heads.)

Napoleon.

I hope that you are satisfied now, Messieurs ! [187]

Caulaincourt.

Sire, this will not do.   It will not be received.

Napoleon.

In heaven's name, why ?

Caulaincourt.

It is not absolute. [188]

Ney.

You abdicate in favour of your son, Sire. [189]

Macdonald.

And you appoint the Empress to be regent. [190]

Caulaincourt.

And, Sire——

Napoleon.

(*Fiercely.*)

Away !   Why do you not direct me
To abdicate in favour of the Bourbons,
And be done with it ?   I abdicate for France ;
And not to make way for the immediate
Return of Louis the Eighteenth !   No !   No !   My
Son shall sit upon my Imperial throne.

Macdonald.

But, Sire, your words are vague.   " The Emperor
   declares

That he is *ready to descend* from the throne."
That will not do.   That is no abdication,
But merely an expression of readiness. [191]

Ney.

The Allies will not entertain any such——[192]

Napoleon.

I am not abdicating at the instance
Nor on the terms of any of the Allies.
It is to Frenchmen that I address my words :
It is to save France from bloody civil war.
Go with this paper to the Provisional
Government, for I shall sign no other—no !

Caulaincourt.

And failing to secure acceptance for it ?

Napoleon.

Be men again !   Appear before your soldiers !
They burn to strike another blow for glory.

Ney.

As I shall show before I die, no other [193]
Loves you as I do, Sire.   You know that my love
For your person is equal to my love for
France.   Can I say more ?   Then by that love I
    swear,
That if you draw your sword, I shall draw my sword,
But prove myself thereby the foe of Frenchmen.

Napoleon.

Go! And return immediately—my friends.

> (NAPOLEON *affectionately embraces them. They*
> *reach the door.*)

Hold! Give me back that fatal abdication!
I utterly repudiate it. It is [194]
False! I am the Emperor. My loyal Guard [195]
Lies camped about me, mighty, invincible!
Let me appear upon that balcony, and
With a look I can arouse those old watch-dogs
Of mine into a fury that would lick up
The Allies, were they ten million strong. Give me
The abdication! I am Emperor still!

> (*The* MARSHALS *bow, filled with emotion, but they*
> *do not give back the paper.* **Exeunt.**
> (NAPOLEON *falls into a reverie before the fire.*)

Enter CONSTANT *on tip-toe.*

Constant.

(*In a whisper to* RUSTAN.)

He means to kill himself. Be quick and help me. [196]

> (CONSTANT *unloads the pistols, and gives the Ara-*
> *bian poniard to* RUSTAN, *who hides it. They*
> *search for other weapons.*)

If he stirs, call me. I shall be close at hand.

> (*Exit* CONSTANT.

Napoleon.

Rustan, tell Constant to come here.

Rustan.

>   At once, Sire.
>   (*Exit* Rustan.

Napoleon.

Berthier a traitor !   Marmont as good as lost !
Murat and Caroline, Talleyrand, Fouché !
And these who yet remain are cowards, cowards !
Where is young France ?   Young France is here,
    eagerly
Waiting for me to lead it on to glory ! [197]
These Marshals are all men stuffed with successes,
All surfeited with honours.   But there are men,
One hundred thousand young men around me now.
I will appeal to them !
>   (*Drums and marching heard.*)
>   Hark !   The Guards go by !
>   (*He springs to the balcony—they cheer.*)

Enter Constant *and* Rustan.

Constant.

You have commands, Sire?

Napoleon.

>   Constant, the *Aide-de-Camp*
On duty will go at once to Marmont's corps [193]
And summon Marmont instantly.   Go at once !
>   (*Exit* Constant.

>   (*More drums are heard.*)

It would be sacrilege to falter while those
Hearts beat. Old Guard! Old battalions of hon-
    our!

Enter CONSTANT.

Constant, the *Aide-de-Camp*, has he returned yet?

Constant.

He has this moment gone, Sire—

Napoleon.

                        Malediction!
Then send another *Aide-de-Camp* after him.
Why do you stand there, fool?   Do as I tell you.
                        (*Exit* CONSTANT.
Now we shall see whether a petty handful
Of Russian slaves, of Bourbon exiles, Prussian
Thieves, can overturn the will of Destiny !

Enter MARSHALS NEY *and* MACDONALD, *and* CAULAIN-
        COURT.

Napoleon.

Well? Well? You look like baffled lovers, not
    men.

Macdonald.

Sire, it is as we all feared——

Ney.

            Abdication !

Caulaincourt.

Absolute abdication without recourse.

Napoleon.

Ha! ha! ha! ha! ha! ha! ha! ha! Old women!
Out! Out! Out! Out! you pack of chicken-
   livers!

Caulaincourt.

There is no argument in calling bad names,
Sire—the facts are as we state them. It is now
For you to say whether the fields of sunny
France shall once more swim with the blood of
   Frenchmen.
You abdicate, or civil war must follow.

Napoleon.

And I suppose that you have taken good care
To make your timely bow to the new powers!
What was the ceremony? Were you compelled
To kiss Monsieur de Talleyrand's fat hand?

Ney.

                                    Sire!

Macdonald.

Sire, we three came to a very different
Conclusion.   Outside that door there, the moment
That we left you, we took an oath upon our
Sword-hilts, Sire——

Napoleon.

          " To let your beards grow and take the
Dagger ? " [199] Corsicans take that oath, Macdonald,
When perfidy beyond the common tempts them.

Caulaincourt.

Sire, the oath we took upon our sword-hilts was
That, come what would, we would obey your orders
To the last.   Yes! give the word, and we shall stand
Once more before the loyal columns of our
Men, and we shall follow you!   We shall not shrink,
Nor fail, nor cry for quarter ; but strike, strike, strike,
Until there is not left a living man to
Strike for you!

Napoleon.

Stop! Caulaincourt, stop! I cannot
Meet such gratitude, such loyalty.   Traitors
I can defy—but in this hour, a friend is
More than I can grapple with.   You took that oath?
And you, too, Ney?
(*They bow assent.*)
And you, Macdonald?

Macdonald.

Yes, Sire!

Napoleon.

Dictate, then, what you will and I will sign it.
To the remotest generation let men [30]
Know, that they were liars all who ever said,
That I loved myself first, my country last.   No!
It was to make France glorious, that I have
Single-handed battled against the world.   And
Now that France prefers to shrivel up into

The paltry territory allowed her by
Her enemies, I must submit.   Dictate, Ney!

Ney.

Command, Sire, what you will except this duty.

Napoleon.

I will with my own hand show France my heart-ache.
Give me the paper—the one I sent to them.
    (*They return the first abdication—he reads it.*)
To what did they object most strenuously?

Ney.

To the provision that your son succeed you.

Napoleon.

Oh! Josephine! It was because you could not
Bear a son, that I divorced you.   The Empress
Who supplanted you bore me this son, and now
The irony of Fate compels me to—
    (*Breaks down.*)

Caulaincourt.
                                Sire!
Napoleon.

Come—come, an end of this! They wish no more
    than
That I abdicate?—My person, what will be
Done with me? Attended you to this—trifle? [301]

Macdonald.

Sire, your dignity and safety were our first

Thought. The imperial title will remain
Your own, and Elba will be recognized by
All the powers as your dominion.

Napoleon.

Elba?

(*Muses a long while.*)
Elba, you say, Macdonald? If I mistake [302]
Not, it is a place of great strategic strength.
Yes, Elba will do. Strategy! Strategy!
(*He writes the abdication.*)
But, Caulaincourt, did you explain to them my
Overtures? Did you not show them that even
Yet I can collect our men and drive the whole
Force of the enemy beyond the Rhine? [303]

Caulaincourt.

Yes,
Sire, I did.

Napoleon.

And they said what?

Caulaincourt.

They laughed, they jeered.

Napoleon.

Who? Who, Caulaincourt, rejected scornfully?

Caulaincourt.

Fouché! [304]

Napoleon.

Again Fouché? If but to blast him—
I will *not* abdicate! God's wounds! Am I to
Be jeered at by hell's own vermin? Perdition!

Macdonald.

Sire, the moments fly. France looks to you for help.

Napoleon.

And not in vain, Macdonald. Take it. It is
My absolute, my fatal abdication.[205]
>   (*He collapses into the chair. The three* GENERALS
>   *withdraw sorrowfully.* RUSTAN *steals out
>   secretly.*)[206]
The sun has set. Josephine's soul breaks now from
Out this pestilential prison-house of Earth,
And darkness everlasting falls upon me.
It must be death!
>   (*He takes one of the pistols out of the case.*)
>   Why did I not die that day
At Arcis-sur-Aube? Or at the fatal bridge
At Arcola?[207]
>   (*He examines the pistol.*)
>   Not loaded yet? That villain
Plays unconsciously into the hands of Fate.
Powder and ball are powerless against me.
>   (*Throws away the pistol.*)
It were ungrateful, too, to pass into the
Everlasting consolation of the night[208]

Without some word of courage to poor Marie.
The love of woman only keeps God on earth.
    (*Writes hastily.*)
And to the Empress, also, should I now write.
She has done nobly well.   She has borne the son
For whom I wedded her, and she has never
In her life complained : therefore she is indeed
A perfect woman. [309]
    (*Writes to her.*)
              To Josephine—I go !
    (*Rises and looks for the poniard.   Finds that*
        Rustan is not at his post.)
Rustan fled also ?   Then loyalty is dead.
Then it must be the poison which I have had [310]
Secreted on my person all these long years !
Close to my heart I have hugged Death's own image,
    (*Takes a small pouch out from his breast.*)
Knowing the hour would come when I should need a
Friend.   That hour has come !
    (*Takes the poison.*)
              Into the hands of God !
    (*He crosses himself—sinks upon the sofa—night*
        falls.   After a few minutes the agony caused
        by the poison begins.)

        Enter Constant.

        Constant.

Merciful heavens !   The Emperor is dead !
    (*At the door.*)

Help! help!　Somebody fetch Doctor Yvan![211]
　　(*He returns and tries to rouse* Napoleon.)
Sire! Sire! It is Constant who speaks.　Sire, awake!

Enter Yvan, Caulaincourt, *and* Attendants.

Yvan.

Is it a wound? a shot?　Who knows about it?
Undo his clothing instantly.　Begone, you!
　　　　　　　　　　　　　　　(*Servants exeunt.*

Constant.

With Monsieur's pardon, it is not any wound.
The Emperor has taken poison.

Yvan.

Poison?

Constant.

From this bag which he wore always hung about
His neck.　Smell it!　Examine it!　I always
Feared that it contained some deadly chemical.

Yvan.

I gave it to the Emperor myself some [212]
Time ago.　It must have lost much of its power.
Air, there—open the window, so!　And, Constant,
Bring my medicines at once—the black camp-chest
Which my valet will give you.　Quick!
　　(*They raise* Napoleon *and try to revive him.*)

Napoleon.

(*Partially conscious.*)　　　　　　　　Caulaincourt!

Caulaincourt.

What have you done, Sire?

Napoleon.

You see I cannot die! [213]
They have been tampering with Death, and Death has
Joined the Bourbons and will not help me. Yvan!

Yvan.

It is I, Sire. How are you feeling now, Sire?

Napoleon.

Give me your arm! So.
(*Rises.*)
Take me to Josephine!

Caulaincourt.

You are not well enough yet, Sire.

Yvan.

To-morrow.
(*Bugles are heard.*)

Napoleon.

They change the watch. The Guard! The Guard!
I hear them.
(*Tries to go to the window.*)

Caulaincourt.

There is to be a grand review to morrow.[214]

Napoleon.

Till then, I beg you leave me. I shall not die.
Go, Caulaincourt, Yvan. Leave me, I pray you.
(YVAN *motions to* CAULAINCOURT *and they quietly
go out. Drums are heard.*)

Napoleon.

(*Going to the balcony.*)
Farewell ! Farewell ! Your Emperor says farewell !
(*He returns to the fireplace.*)

CURTAIN.

NOTES.

[1] Napoleon with his wife and immediate attendants went to Malmaison on Sunday, March 18, 1804, and remained there one week. It was on the night of the 20th that D'Enghien was shot. (*Thiers : Consulate and the Empire.*) For the substantial accuracy of this scene, consult *Thiers, Saint-Amand, Bourrienne, and De Rémusat.*

[2] Napoleon shut himself up alone; would speak to no one; wrote no letters. (*Thiers.*)

[3] Napoleon, noticing Mme. de Rémusat's paleness, said to her: "Why didn't you rouge?" (*De Rémusat.*)

[4] "My mother was in tears." (*Eugène de Beauharnais.*)

[5] "Nothing can equal the stupor which reigned at Malmaison." (*Pasquier.*)

[6] Sir Walter Scott's account of the 18th Brumaire gives the details of Lucien Bonaparte's very effective assistance. (*Life of Napoleon.*)

"Lucien was in the habit of reminding him of them [his services] in an aggressive manner." (*De Rémusat.*)

[7] Many years after this, when Napoleon was at the zenith, Lucien rejected tempting offers with the words: "My principles are still the same." (*D'Abrantès.*)

[8] Pasquier, without hesitation, calls the execution of D'Enghien "a murder." (*Memoirs.*)

[9] Referring to the plot of Georges Cadoudal, and the episode of the "Infernal Machine." (*Thiers et al.*)

[10] "Must I rely on myself? I shall suffice!" (*De Rémusat.*)

" He only can protect himself, etc." (*D'Abrantès.*)

[11] I owe this conceit to Saint Amand. (*The Wife of the First Consul.*)

[12] Saint-Amand's is a most graphic account of the scene of D'Enghien's execution. (*Wife of the First Consul.*)

[13] It seemed the more revolting duty to impose upon Caulaincourt, in that he was "attached by consanguinity to the ex-royal family, and especially to the Condés." (*Thiers.*)

[14] Napoleon sent Real the night before the execution with sealed orders which would have delayed that fatal conclusion; by an errour the message was not delivered until it was too late. (*Thiers.*)

[15] "From that moment [when on D'Enghien's death, Napoleon determined to become Emperor] a cloud hangs over his star. . . . Josephine had a presentiment of this. . . . filled her with a secret dread." (*Saint-Amand.*)

[16] The use of "Citizen" and "Citizeness" ended in a few weeks after this. Napoleon formally discarded the use on May 18. 1804. (*De Rémusat.*)

[17] Constant speaks of his difficulty in shaving Napoleon, having frequently almost cut him, etc., etc. (*Memoirs*)

[18] Josephine says: "I hung about his neck," etc. (*Saint-Amand.*)

[19] Four years before this Josephine had said "I beg of you, don't be a King!" (*Saint-Amand.*)

[20] Napoleon's words were: "This is not women's business." (*Pasquier.*)

[21] See Napoleon's Letters (to Josephine), and especially those written in his earlier campaigns, for evidences of his jealousy.

[22] As to the errour, see note 14.

[23] Napoleon's expression *verbatim.* (*Thiers.*)

[24] Josephine passed a troubled night. "She became hysterical," and plied Napoleon with anxious questions. (*Pasquier.*)

[25] Napoleon's very words: "My star arose at Arcola." (*Saint-Amand.*)

[26] For the various sentiments here expressed see Napoleon's *Letters.*

[27] "Imagination rules the world;" words used by Napoleon at St. Helena.

[28] The First Consul had by degrees ignored the other two Consuls, as well as the constitutional legislature; but Napoleon was uneasy in lawlessness. (*Thiers, Scott.*)

[29] Poor Caulaincourt was at once held in the most unjust contempt. (*De Rémusat.*)

[30] As a soldier Caulaincourt manfully obeyed—against his natural instincts and personal feelings. (*Thiers.*)

[31] This refers to the letter which Real failed to deliver. (See Note 14 *supra.*)

[32] "D'Enghien's blood must remain indelibly upon Napoleon." (*Scott.*)

[33] Caulaincourt, according to Mme. de Rémusat, was one of that "small number who told Napoleon the truth." (*Memoirs.*)

[34] This was undoubtedly Napoleon's object. (*Scott.*)

[35] Caulaincourt was extremely sad when ordered to arrest D'Enghien. (*Thiers.*)

[36] "He expressed his indignation so forcibly," says Pasquier, on this occasion, "that those present hardly knew what countenance to assume." (*Memoirs.*)

[37] All of Napoleon's sisters intrigued against Josephine. (*De Rémusat.*)

[38] Mme. Murat had many grievances against Josephine, soon to grow into mortal hatred owing to the slights shown by the Emperor. (*Thiers, Saint-Amand, et al.*)

[39] This slander was assiduously spread. (*Saint-Amand.*) Utterly without foundation. (*Sir Walter Scott.*)

[40] " . . . . here was public opinion escaping from his hold." (*De Rémusat.*)

[41] On the relations of Fouché and Talleyrand to Napoleon

and to each other, consult Pasquier's finely discriminating study. (*Memoirs.*)

[42] Napoleon said this of Metternich. (*De Rémusat.*) Fouché favoured the immediate setting up of the Empire. (*Thiers.*)

[43] Pasquier calls Talleyrand, "Chaplain of all the immoralities." (*Memoirs.*)

[44] One of Talleyrand's recorded *bon-mots*. (*De Rémusat.*)

[45] Chateaubriand resigned on the day following. (*De Rémusat.*)

[46] This tirade against Talleyrand was literally pronounced by Napoleon. (*Pasquier.*)

[47] Napoleon to the last charged Talleyrand with having secretly urged the execution of D'Enghien. (*Las Cases and O'Meara.*)

[48] Napoleon complained that it was "hard to find in one's own family such stubborn opposition . . . [but] you, Josephine,—you will be my comfort always." (*De Rémusat.*)

[49] Precisely such an offer was made by Napoleon to Lucien at a subsequent time, and in like manner was it refused. (*D'Abrantès.*)

[50] This was literally Lucien's speech and action. (*D'Abrantès.*)

[51] The Pope was lodged in that wing of the Tuileries called the Pavilion of Flora. (*Thiers.*)

[52] Napoleon fairly snatched the crown to prevent the Pope from crowning him. (*Thiers, Saint-Amand.*)

[53] It was a chief claim of the Mediæval Papacy, that earthly crowns were at its bestowal. (*Bryce's Holy Roman Empire.*)

[54] Nothing is more unusual than for a Pope to leave Rome. Pius VII. did so against the advice of his cardinals, and with fear and trembling. (*Thiers, Scott.*)

[55] —Josephine dated Napoleon's overthrow from the assumption of the imperial crown. (*Saint-Amand.*) She said, "I knew he was lost from the hour he made himself Emperor." (*Bourrienne.*)

[56] " . . . the moment which dispelled all her incessant dread of divorce," was that in which Josephine was crowned by Napoleon. (*Saint-Amand.*)

[57] An ancient title of the Popes.

[58] Talleyrand was formerly Bishop of Autun. (*Thiers.*)

[59] Napoleon's sisters, Caroline and Pauline, out of envious spite, dropped Josephine's train at the very altar, and a serious break would have occurred had not Napoleon sternly rebuked them then and there. (*Saint-Amand.*)

[60] The question of the succession, while technically settled among the nephews of Napoleon, was never accepted as final, and proved the cause of bitter family dissensions. (*De Rémusat.*)

[61] By law the priest of the parish must witness a marriage. On the whole matter see a note giving authorities in *Bourrienne*. (*Memoirs*, Vol. II.)

[62] The Pope was scandalized on learning that Napoleon and Josephine had never been ecclesiastically married. (*Thiers.*)

[63] They were secretly married at the Tuileries by Cardinal Fesch on the eve of the coronation, Talleyrand and Berthier being the only witnesses. (*Thiers.*)

[64] Saint-Amand gives a detailed description of the coronation robes, and also the dress of the court pages, etc. (*Court of the Empress Josephine :* SCRIBNER'S.)

[65] To the lasting credit of Cardinal Fesch, he sided throughout with the Pope against his all-powerful nephew. (*Bourrienne.*)

[66] Josephine became devoutly attached to the Pope. (*Pasquier.*)

[67] The Pope wore a plain white woollen cassock. (*De Rémusat.*)

[68] The quarrel between the Pope and Napoleon broke out at once. (*Pasquier.*)

[69] Napoleon had solemnly promised to allow the Pope to crown him. (*Saint-Amand.*)

[10] See Sir Walter Scott's account of the Papal relation to coronations. (*Life of Napoleon.*)

[11] The Pope's contention was just. See the letter of Cardinal Consalvi, quoted by Saint-Amand. (*Josephine.*)

[12] Ségur was the Grand Master of Ceremonies, but Talleyrand was looked upon as the authority on all points of etiquette. (*De Rémusat.*)

[13] For the Coronation ceremonies and the reconstruction of the Court, the whole literature of etiquette was ransacked. (*Saint-Amand.*)

[14] The Pope always called Josephine "our dear daughter." (*Saint-Amand.*)

[15] Josephine pleaded, in some instances successfully, for the pardon of those who were implicated in the conspiracies unearthed shortly before the coronation. (*Thiers, De Rémusat, et al.*)

[16] Napoleon retired from his wretched winter-quarters at Osterode to the castle of Finkenstein the first of April, 1807, and there received the beautiful Polish Countess Walewska. (*Bourrienne.*)

[17] Napoleon speaks of the comfort of his open fires at Finkenstein. (*Letters to Josephine.*)

[18] Napoleon sent to Warsaw for Mme. Walewska. (*Constant.*)

[19] His valet complains of the difficulty of shaving Napoleon, but boasts, nevertheless, that he never cut him. (*Constant.*)

[80] It pleased Napoleon to find that his blundering orders, given when absent-minded, were not obeyed. (*Bourrienne.*)

[81] This part of the scene is from lively details given by Saint-Amand. (*Josephine.*)

[82] Bourrienne gives account of the meeting of Napoleon and Countess Walewska at a ball in Warsaw as does Mme. de Rémusat. (*Memoirs.*)

[83] Napoleon had a fine apartment at Finkenstein, adjoining his own, fitted up for his mistress. (*Bourrienne.*)

[84] The Duchess of Abrantès loyally denies that Junot, her husband, was tale-bearer; but he is commonly thought to have advised Napoleon of Josephine's light conduct. (*Memoirs.*)

[85] Napoleon's orders were, that only bad news should be told him at night—good news could wait. (*Bourrienne.*)

[86] To the privileged valet we are indebted for our knowledge of the bearing and nature of this most pathetic and lovable girl. (*Constant.*)

[87] It has been hoped in this song to catch the spirit of the Polish heart—the weird-warm mixture of a northern race with a southern soul.

[88] Josephine accused Napoleon during this absence of not reading her letters, a charge from which he defends himself. (*Letters.*)

[89] This summer of 1807 was the high-noon of the Empire. On August 15th (Napoleon's birthday) a splendid *fête* was given at Fontainebleau. (*Saint-Amand.*)

[90] The loving Mme. de Rémusat was all for peace and good-will. (*Letter of Talleyrand, De Rémusat.*)

[91] I owe the phrase to *Saint-Amand.* (*Josephine.*)

[92] The little son of Hortense and Louis Bonaparte, then queen and king of Holland, had died only a few months before, namely, on the 5th May, 1807. (*Saint-Amand.*

[93] Refers to the wretched married life of Hortense. (*De Rémusat.*)

[94] Napoleon honoured Hortense above all women. (*De Rémusat.*)

[95] This devotion to the girl led scandal mongers to attribute it to a criminal relation with her. Sir Walter Scott, no lover of Napoleon, meets all these charges against Napoleon's family life with scornful denials. (*Life of Napoleon,* also, *De Rémusat.*)

[96] Napoleon's other amours were very transient affairs. (*Scott.*)

[97] Countess Walewska was, according to Mme. Junot,

"the only woman Napoleon ever really loved." (*Memoirs.*)

[98] Napoleon actually introduced Mme. Walewska at Court, and provided quarters for her at Saint Cloud. (*De Rémusat.*)

[99] Almost literally Napoleon's complaint. (*Saint-Amand.*)

[100] Mme. Murat was the first to discern the Emperor's relations with Countess Walewska, and made good use of her knowledge in her back stairs warfare. (*De Rémusat.*)

[101] Napoleon, unlike his Bourbon predecessors, believed in kings publicly appearing virtuous. (*Las Cases.*)

[102] The gallantries of M. de Talleyrand are historical. (*Pasquier.*)

[103] See the terrible record of duplicity and shame given by Chancellor Pasquier. (*Memoirs.*)

[104] Mme. Murat had succeeded in "fascinating M. Fouché," and was "worming out of him" the points she needed. (*De Rémusat.*)

[105] Napoleon's exact words : "as sweet to me as Josephine's voice." (*Saint-Amand.*)

[106] It was Mme. de Staël who asked these questions and received these answers, at the ball at which she first met Napoleon. (*Mme. de Staël.*)

[107] Napoleon's very words, spoken at Helena. (*Las Cases.*)

[108] "Europe is a mole hill," said Napoleon. (*Saint-Amand.*)

[109] See *Saint-Amand.* (*Citizeness Beauharnais.*)

[110] From a letter of Napoleon to Louis in 1807.

[111] "Louis XVIII. is a principle." (*Bourrienne.*)

[112] Napoleon on his death-bed said, "Not every one who would be, is an atheist." (*Antomarchi's Supplement to Las Cases.*)

[113] "That sacramental phrase, 'My Policy,'" was all-powerful. (*De Rémusat.*)

[114] Josephine began calling Napoleon "Sire," at this time. (*Saint-Amand.*)

[115] Rumours of divorce were now general. (*Mme. Junot.*)

[116] Napoleon called Fouché " a miscreant of all colours." (*Memorial of St. Helena.*)

[117] I owe the phrase to Mme. Junot, who applied it to Napoleon. (*Memoirs.*)

[118] " Hortense makes me believe in virtue," said Napoleon. (*Saint-Amand.*)

[119] This is a literal translation of the note written by Napoleon. (*De Rémusat.*)

[120] Just such a nocturnal expedition was undertaken by Josephine and Mme. de Rémusat—without results. (*De Rémusat.*)

[121] Josephine's very words as to Rustan. (*De Rémusat.*)

[122] Talleyrand's life, according to Pasquier, was " consecrated to obscure intrigues." (*Memoirs.*)

[123] Napoleon's son by Countess Walewska was born in Paris (*De Rémusat*), and went with his mother to visit Napoleon at Elba. (*Sir Walter Scott.*)

[124] Napoleon made just such a proposition to Josephine. (*De Rémusat.*)

[125] The famous Corvisart refused as a physician to countenance the infamous hoax. (*De Rémusat.*)

[126] On another occasion Napoleon said that " love is a passion which sets all the universe on one side, and on the other the beloved object." (*De Rémusat.*)

[127] It was in a gallery with embrasured windows at Fontainebleau that Fouché made the fatal announcement to Josephine. (*Scott.*)

[128] A *mot* indicative of his character is Fouché's famous : " It is worse than a crime—it is a blunder." (*Scott.*)

[129] Napoleon himself declared that he would be unable to be firm in the face of Josephine's affliction. (*De Rémusat.*)

[130] No doubt there was reason in the feeling, that an heir was essential to the Imperial fortunes. (*Thiers.*)

[131] " I am your wife," was Josephine's sufficient argument. (*De Rémusat.*)

[132] " I shall never have the strength to oblige you to leave me," confessed Napoleon. (*De Rémusat.*)

[133] Napoleon used these words speaking of Josephine at St. Helena. (*Las Cases.*)

[134] I borrow the phrase from Saint-Amand. (*Memoirs.*)

[135] Napoleon's letters to Josephine teem with cruel charges born of his jealous nature.

[136] For some years Napoleon was indeed the more ardent lover of the two. (*Saint-Amand.*)

[137] There were not wanting those to keep the absent Napoleon posted in the scandals at home. (*Mme. Junot.*)

[138] According to the Duchess of Abrantès there is no doubt of Josephine's intrigue with M. Charles. Pasquier, moreover, substantiates the charge of her immorality, and speaks of Josephine's infidelities in the plural. (*Memoirs.*)

[139] " Just ten days after," says Sir Walter Scott. (*Life of Napoleon.*)

[140] It had not been decided yet that the Austrian Princess, Marie Louise, was to supplant Josephine. (*Thiers.*)

[141] Such was Napoleon's superstitious, but very real, belief as to his relations to Josephine. (*Thiers, Pasquier, et al.*)

[142] Napoleon's very words—stranger yet, his very belief. (*De Rémusat.*)

[143] This is a literal extract from the letter written at Verona, November, 1796. (*Bourrienne.*)

[144] For these details see Bourrienne. (*Memoirs.*)

[145] Extracts from a letter written on November 28, 1806, while Napoleon was in Poland. (*Saint-Amand.*)

[146] One of Napoleon's generals testified to the influence of the beauties of Poland over the French officers. (*Savary.*)

[147] These words are from a letter written by Napoleon at Porto Maurizio, April 3d, 1796. (*Saint-Amand.*)

[148] From a long letter written at Tortona, June 15, 1796. (*Saint-Amand.*)

[149] " He caught Josephine in his arms, and told her, in a

burst of tenderness, that he should never have the strength to part from her." (*Thiers.*)

[150] The *Moniteur* for December 17, 1809, contains the sublimely pathetic words of Josephine by which she offered herself in sacrifice to France, to "his policy," and to her devotion to her husband. (Quoted by *Scott*, note.)

[151] For the official form of Josephine's self renunciation, consult Sir Walter Scott. (*Life of Napoleon.*)

[152] "She fell into a long and profound swoon." (*Scott.*)

[153] Read Saint-Amand on Malmaison. (*Court of the Empress.*)

[154] After Josephine's divorce she became reconciled to the Countess Walewska and received her at Malmaison. (*De Rémusat.*)

[155] The troubled nights, bad dreams, and dark hours of the outcast Empress have been graphically pictured. (*Avrillion.*)

[156] On her death-bed Josephine said: "Napoleon is in distress and I cannot be with him." (*Saint-Amand.*)

[157] Caulaincourt was devoted to Josephine.

[158] The Allies entered Paris on March 30, 1814, the capitulation was signed at two in the morning of the 31st. (*D'Abrantès.*)

[159] On his way to Paris Napoleon met General Belliard a few miles from the city, at an inn called La Cour de France, retreating with his cavalry. After learning of the complete overthrow he went back to Fontainebleau. (*Scott.*)

[160] Caulaincourt was sent to Paris to beg terms from the triumphant Allies. (*Scott.*)

[161] This was a small apartment up-stairs chosen by Napoleon. The little yellow sofa and mahogany table are historical. (*Bourrienne, Saint-Amand, etc.*)

[162] Save that the Duke of Bassano was also present, our scene is true to the facts. (*Bourrienne, Junot, Scott, Hazlitt, et al.*)

[163] The very words spoken to Napoleon. (*D'Abrantès.*)

[164] The action of the Marshals was brave and loyal. (*Bourrienne.*)

[165] Macdonald performed this great feat. (*D'Abrantès.*)

[166] Napoleon was immensely outnumbered. (*Thiers.*)

[167] These impulsive orders were given by Napoleon under the sting of chagrin and thwarted ambition (*Scott.*)

[168] Marmont's defection is a most interesting episode, and it would seem that he was not a traitor. (*Bourrienne.*)

[169] The case of Berthier was different. He assured Napoleon of his devotion, and the same day made his weak submission to the new government. (*D'Abrantès.*)

[170] "Caulaincourt, Mankind! mankind!" exclaimed Napoleon. (*Saint-Amand.*)

[171] Berthier was made a Marshal, Prince of Wagram, and Prince of Neufchâtel, and was at Napoleon's side always. Many years later he committed suicide through remorse. (*Thiers.*)

[172] Murat, King of Naples, was counted upon to defend the northeastern frontiers. He proved a traitor. (*Thiers.*)

[173] "It was she (Caroline) who perhaps dealt him the final blow." (*Pasquier.*)

[174] Read Thiers on this point. (*Consulate and Empire.*)

[175] When the Allies entered Paris Talleyrand remained and was very soon found useful to them. He became the head of the Provisional Government. (*Scott, Thiers, Bourrienne, et al.*)

[176] Fouché found it easy to change masters. (*Bourrienne.*)

[177] The careless Parisians were ready for the change. (*Scott, Thiers.*)

[178] Napoleon's vacillation was natural and no proof of insincerity.

[179] "The act may be regarded as the noblest in Napoleon's life." (*Junot.*)

[180] "A little while—or six years." Napoleon's expression. (*Bourrienne.*)

[181] "In politics there is no resurrection." (*De Rémusat.*)

[182] This was an Arabian poniard which Napoleon ordered Constant to place near him. (*D'Abrantès.*)

[183] Napoleon gave Constant 50,000 francs at this time for the purpose mentioned. (*D'Abrantès*, note.)

[184] "If I had not forsaken her, fortune would not have failed me," groaned Napoleon. (*Saint-Amand.*)

[185] Josephine died a few weeks after this, on May 29th, 1814.

[186] Napoleon's very words. (*Bourrienne.*)

[187] "Here, gentlemen! are you satisfied?" said Napoleon. (*Bourrienne.*)

[188] Napoleon's phrase left a way to retreat. (*Thiers.*)

[189] Napoleon said in the first abdication, that the "welfare of the country . . . is inseparable from the rights of his [my] son." (*Thiers.*)

[190] The abdication provided for the Regency of the Empress. (*Thiers.*)

[191] "Ready to descend" was not conclusive. (*Bourrienne.*)

[192] The Allies rejected this abdication. (*Scott.*)

[193] Marshal Ney was shot for having supported Napoleon on his return from Elba. (*Thiers.*)

[194] Napoleon recalled even this half-useless paper. (*Bourrienne.*)

[195] "The Guard remained loyal." (*D'Abrantès.*)

[196] Historically correct. Constant, fearing suicidal intentions on Napoleon's part, hid the weapons. Another valet, one Marchand, helped him. (*D'Abrantès.*)

[197] The young inferior officers would have eagerly rallied. (*Scott.*)

[198] Napoleon issued these orders excitedly. (*Bourrienne.*)

[199] A Corsican oath. (*D'Abrantès.*)

[200] It was for France that Napoleon felt he suffered. (*Thiers.*)

[201] The Marshals stipulated for Napoleon's personal safety and dignity. (*Thiers.*)

[202] On hearing of Elba, Napoleon became keenly interested in its geography and military features. (*Scott.*)

[203] After Waterloo Napoleon offered still to drive the enemy out of France with the broken remnants of his army. (*Saint-Amand.*)

[204] It was Fouché who mockingly declined Napoleon's offers. (*Saint-Amand.*)

[205] The second form of abdication was unconditional and irrecoverable. (*Thiers, Scott.*)

[206] Rustan, the Mameluke slave, stealthily fled from the sinking ship of Napoleon. (*Bourrienne.*)

[207] Why did I not die at Arcis-sur-Aube?" said Napoleon. (*Saint-Amand.*)

[208] He wrote to his nearest friends. (*Bourrienne.*)

[209] Of Marie Louise, Napoleon spoke kindly. (*Thiers.*)

[210] This poison Napoleon had kept in a little bag around his neck. It was Prussic acid. (*D'Abrantès.*)

[211] Dr. Yvan was in attendance that night. (*Junot, Hazlitt.*)

[212] It was Dr. Corvisart who gave it to Napoleon. (*Junot*)

[213] " You see that I cannot die," complained Napoleon. (*Junot.*)

[214] Napoleon reviewed the Guard at Fontainebleau and took a pathetic farewell of the Eagles. (*Scott, Thiers, et al.*)